WOLFER

G·K
Hall
&Co.

WOlfeR

MAC McKEE

G.K. Hall & Co.
Thorndike, Maine

Copyright © 1995 by Mac McKee

Published in 1998 by arrangement with The Wilshire Literary Agency.

G.K. Hall Large Print Western Series.

The text of this Large Print edition is unabridged.
Other aspects of the book may vary from the original edition.

Set in 16 pt. Plantin by Al Chase.

Printed in the United States on permanent paper.

Library of Congress Cataloging in Publication Data
McKee, Mac.
    Wolfer / Mac McKee.
      p.   cm.
    ISBN 0-7838-8435-4 (lg. print : hc : alk. paper)
    1. Human-animal relationships — West (U.S.) — Fiction.
    2. Wolves — West (U.S.) — Fiction. 3. Large type books.
    I. Title.
    [PS3563.C3744W65   1998]
    813'.54—dc21   97-52951

To
Kathy, Glenna and Shirley
who tore my book apart
and helped me put it back together,

and

To the best agent
a writer ever had,
Carol McCleary,

I love you all.

Chapter One

A wry smile deepened the crow's feet darting from Roan McCrae's sky-blue eyes as he sighted down the barrel of the .44 Winchester.

"Just a little bit more," he breathed, "and I'll have five more cartwheels to jingle in me pockets."

Fifty yards downwind from Roan, the wolf threw its shaggy head into the air and sniffed, inching further from the boulder's protective cover.

It caught sight of the deer carcass hanging as a lure and lunged from its hiding place. It hadn't surged forward the length of its own body before the heavy slug from the Winchester slammed its life away.

A splash of gray hit the brush a few feet from the downed wolf. Within a heartbeat, Roan worked the rifle lever and aimed again, but the single glimpse was all he got. After a minute of tensed waiting, he lowered the gun and walked toward his kill.

"About what I figured," he said, studying the dead animal. "Ain't much more than a whelp. You should've listened to your ma, boy. She wouldn't have dashed out like that no matter how hungry she be. She'd have circled around until she got a whiff of me as well. Ain't too many beasties smarter than a bitch wolf. Ah well, five dollars for a whelp spends the same as five dollars for a full-grown one, I'd be thinking."

He reached for the skinning knife in its sheath on the back of his belt. Holding the wolf's ear, he deftly sliced upward then across the forehead. Two cuts, an inch apart, yielded both ears, held together by the strip of flesh.

Roan's camp was a half mile upwind from where he had strung the deer carcass. With the ears deposited in a smelly grain sack, he returned to his digs, broke camp and headed for town.

"Faith," he said. "Time I be cashing in."

The Last Stand Saloon was always busiest on Saturday. This one was no exception.

Five men sat at a table and supplied their share of the cacophony in the room, induced by three half-empty whiskey bottles in the center of their table.

One of the five, a wide-shouldered man with a shock of unruly salt and pepper hair matching his drooping handlebar moustache, glanced toward the door as it opened. He smiled and straightened in his chair.

"Boys." He nodded in the door's direction. "We're about to get a report on the current wolf population around here, I think."

All heads turned as Roan shouldered his way toward them. Of average height and stout build, his movements were quick and easy. He removed his battered wide-brimmed hat as he approached the table, and ran his hand through unruly red hair. Light reflected off a few gray strands. Other than that, he appeared to be younger than most in the crowd.

His smile, wide and sincere, revealed a set of even white teeth.

"Roan McCrae, good to see you, boy," the man with the moustache said in greeting. "Sit down if you can find a chair and tell us we ain't going to lose our calf crops from wolves anymore."

"Thank you, Mr. Quade, but I'll be needing to clean up a bit before —"

"Whew." A smartly dressed man next to Quade held his nose. "I should say you do. You stink, man."

"Aye, Mr. Steppe, I'm knowing that." Roan shrugged and turned back to speak to Quade. "I saw your big black out front and figured you would all be here. Just thought I'd come in and collect before you all start homeward."

"How many we owing you for, Roan?"

"Twenty-five."

"Twenty-five!" echoed a small, wiry man across the table. "That's a fair number for the length of time you've been out, Roan."

"Aye, Mr. Capp, guess I'm one of the lucky Irish and a good shot to boot."

"Yeah, maybe," Steppe cut in. "It's hard to believe. You've only been gone a couple weeks."

"I have the proof out there on me saddle and me horse is suffering for it. Would you care to come out and count them, Mr. Steppe?" He hadn't cared for Azle Steppe the first time he met him. He had cared less with each meeting since.

9

"That won't be necessary," Quade replied. "We believe you, Roan."

"Like hell we do!" Steppe shouted, leaping from his chair. "I want to see what I'm paying for. Half of them are probably dog ears."

"Mr. Steppe," Roan began, his tone clearly sarcastic, "would you be knowing the difference?"

"You'll damn sure find out. Lead the way, Mr. *Wolfer*."

Roan shoved his way through the crowd. Once outside, he ducked beneath the hitch rail and untied the tow sack from the saddle.

Just as Azle Steppe moved onto the saloon porch, Roan dumped the contents of the sack at his feet. Azle jumped back and wiped his shoes on the straw mat in the saloon doorway as he would have had he stepped in a pile of manure. He glared at Roan. "I ought to jack your teeth loose for that, you filthy son of Irish trash."

Roan stood spraddle-legged and jabbed a finger at Steppe. "In the first place, Mister Fancy Britches, three like yourself couldn't get close enough to touch me let alone do harm. If you think I speak not the truth, it's your privilege to step down here and try."

Roan retreated a couple of steps and pointed to the ground in front of him.

Steppe sneered. "I wouldn't dirty my hands on the likes of you."

By now, a crowd had gathered. People exited from the saloon and passersby stopped, hoping for a fight.

Roan's face reddened. "You called me a son of Irish trash, sir. I'll have you be knowing I resent that. It's true I wasn't handed down a few thousand beautiful acres of range as yourself was. Me Da was a poor man, so I work for a living. When you work, Mr. Steppe, you sweat and it's unfortunate, but sweat doesn't smell like lilacs."

A raw-boned brute moved to Steppe's side. He sneered at Roan. "I work, too, McCrae, and sweat, but I damn sure don't smell like you. You're nothing but Irish scum."

Roan turned his fury toward the speaker. The look from the man's red-rimmed eyes stopped him. "You've been drinking your fill, fake Tanner. I'll not be taking advantage of a drunk. Stay clear."

"Drunk, am I?" Tanner shouted. "I've heard all I want to hear from your big mouth."

Roan was three long strides away from the saloon porch. Tanner reached him in two and finished the last step with a swinging haymaker.

Roan ducked. He wanted to vent his rage on Azle Steppe, damned coward that he was. But now, already angered, Roan accepted Jake Tanner's challenge. He believed in accepting that which was offered. The big foreman of the Double S would be his quarry.

With all his weight, Roan drove a right into the ranch foreman's hard-muscled gut. Tanner bent forward, his arms closed across his stomach. Without a second's hesitation, Roan slammed upward with his left, straightening Tanner. Blood gushed from his splayed nose.

Roan sneered. "Big tough man." He drove a right, then a left. With each blow, Tanner staggered back toward the crowd. Roan finished the fight with a long roundhouse that ended at Jake Tanner's jaw. Tanner spun like a dust devil.

The crowd parted to let him fall. With a groan, he collapsed across the boardwalk and lay still.

Scarcely winded, Roan dug a soiled bandanna from his hip pocket and stood easy. With slow, deliberate strokes, he wiped Tanner's blood from his knuckles. All the while, he regarded Azle Steppe. "Now, Mr. Steppe, would you tell me if any of those are dog ears?"

"Go to hell!" Steppe replied. He whirled and headed into the saloon.

Roan's voice stopped him. "You owe me twenty-five dollars, Azle Steppe, your share of the bounty, and by heaven, you'll pay it."

Steppe reached into his pocket, pulling out a handful of coins. Selecting a gold double eagle and five silver dollars, he threw them at Roan's feet. "That's the last dollar you'll get from me, you Irish —"

"Ah, ah, ah," Roan warned, wagging his finger.

Steppe spoke to the two men behind him. "Haul Tanner over to that horse trough and dump him. Then get him back out to the ranch." He pointed a finger at Roan, who busied himself retrieving the coins from the dirt. "You! Get this mess of wolf ears off the porch."

"Aye, sir, Mr. Steppe. As you wish, sir. I'll do

it right away, sir." He laughed and added, "When we both get to hell."

Steppe turned and opened the saloon door. "That stupid ass. You coming, Warren?"

Warren Quade, as far as Roan was concerned, was all right. He owned the huge Q-C Ranch which bordered Steppe's Double S to the south. He had expressed his opinion of Steppe more times than Roan cared to count. Quade disliked Steppe intensely, yet they had never exchanged cross words. Roan supposed it was because Steppe knew Quade could crush him financially, buy and sell him at will.

"In a minute, Azle," Quade replied. "I owe this man some money, too."

Roan collected the foul-smelling grain sack from the saloon porch and retied the top of it as Quade handed him a hundred dollar bank note.

"What's this?" Roan asked, wiping his hands on the sides of his pantlegs. "Are you paying for the association now? You owe me only twenty-five."

"I'll collect from the rest. Roan, I think it might be wise if you didn't come back into the saloon tonight."

"And pray tell, why not?"

"Dammit, you know why." Sharpness edged Quade's voice. "Azle and three or four of his boys are still in there. The place would get busted to hell and you'd wind up in jail again. Haven't you seen enough of the inside of those cells these past two years?"

13

Roan sighed and hefted the sack of wolf ears. "Aye, right you are, of course. I'll go bury these things." He moved to the hitch rail and untied the reins of his dun, who eyed the sack in Roan's hand and shied. "Easy, boy, I don't like the smell either. We'll be getting rid of it if you'll just behave."

Two Double S hands rode past leading Jake Tanner's horse with Tanner slumped over the saddlehorn. He turned his head slightly and glared at Roan. "I'll see you again, Irish," he slurred through swollen lips.

"Aye, but you better hope it ain't real soon, Tanner."

Warren Quade's voice drew his attention. "Did you see the lobe?"

"Aye. Twice."

"Are you going back out?"

"Aye. Tomorrow sometime, but tonight I'll purchase a change of clothes, a bath, a steak and a drink of whiskey. In that order." His eyes narrowed as he studied Quade's face. "Don't you be worrying none, Mr. Quade. I'll be buying me whiskey at the Butte. No one you know goes in there."

Quade laughed. "All right, Roan, do that. But stop by my ranch when you're in the area. I want to talk with you."

"The day after tomorrow you'll see me there."

"Fine enough. Good night, Roan. Stay out of trouble."

"You know me, Mr. Quade. I don't go looking for trouble. Neither do I shy away from it."

Chapter Two

Roan rode off the Continental Divide in early afternoon and crossed the South Fork at a high gravel bar. Along the east bank he could travel for miles and never leave Q-C range, which ended at the Dakota reservation boundary.

He hadn't gone far when his progress was halted by a barbed wire fence of four strands, tightly stretched around tough bois d'arc posts. He cupped his hand above his eyes and squinted into the distance. The fence became nothing more than a straight line dividing the greed of man from the freedom of the land. Man was winning.

He turned right and kicked hard at the top strand of wire. It yielded for a moment to the force of his boot heel then sprang stubbornly back to its original tautness.

"Damned shackles!" he said. "You'd manacle the wind if you could. Imprison the beauty of these hills. Ah well, I suppose you're a necessary bit of evil the likes of us free men have to endure, but you'll always be the spawn of Lucifer hisself as far as I'm concerned."

The barbs weren't meant to keep Q-C stock inside. That was a large part of the problem. The bits of razor-sharp metal were designed to tear the flesh of the wild things that might kill a newborn calf. "A creature's got a right to feed itself when it's hungry." He kicked again at the fence. "Don't do you no good to be here anyway. You might keep the likes of a bear away, but the wolves . . . they ain't afraid of you." He slowed his mount and pulled a tuft of gray fur from one of the barbed spindles. "Like I'm telling you, a wolf's smart. She'll go under or over." He raised his voice slightly. "So what the hell good are you?"

Ahead he saw the heavy rails of an iron gate. He rode alongside the gatepost and unfastened the leather thong that held the gate closed.

The better part of an hour later, Roan forded Muledeer Creek and came to an abrupt halt as he caught sight of the tracks. He dismounted and laid his hand over a single paw print. The toes of the wolf's print reached beyond his own palm.

Roan straightened, a frown creasing his brow. "It's Patch all right," he said aloud. "Sure as there's the little people. Damn lobo does cover ground."

Three days before, while cooking his breakfast, Roan had risen suddenly to his feet. A shiver ran down his spine. Eyes watched him. He could feel their wary gaze burning into him. Indians — maybe. The Blackfoot reservation lay not far to the north.

The uncomfortable sensation persisted. Between sips of hot coffee, he scanned his surroundings. Fifty feet to his left grew a copse of quaking aspen. Usually a sight Roan found pleasant, the aspen grove thrust another shudder up his backbone. His neck hairs bristled. Barely visible at the edge of the trees sat the lobo, his eyes focused, unwavering, on Roan.

Roan had seen the big lobo more times than he cared to these past three years, but only for brief moments and at a distance too great to fear.

Roan edged toward his rifle. His hand crept forward, fingers ready to tighten around the butt of the Winchester.

The beast didn't move.

Roan pulled his hand back, leaned against the tree where his rifle rested and glared at the animal.

The wolf's dark gray coat had grown long and shaggy for approaching winter. Three spots on his side and one on his front quarter were as white as the new-fallen snow. Roan nodded. The strange markings were battle scars, areas where the hide had been torn away and regenerated in the new fur color. "Patch," he said and smiled. The name had stuck.

Roan spoke to him, letting his voice cut through the silence. "Once, me boy, I thought you were the leader of those who attacked me Katie. Then I studied the tracks. You would be dead by now had I not. You understand?"

The wolf didn't flick an ear.

"The other tracks I could not identify, so I shoot your kind on sight."

Patch's only response was a slight ripple of his shoulder muscle.

"So why are you here? What is it you want?"

Patch snarled, revealing long white fangs. He

lifted himself to all fours, turned and disappeared into the trees.

Later that evening, four miles from the town of Buckhorn, Roan had sighted the wolf again. "Faith, are you following me?" he asked, but the wolf disappeared over a knoll.

Now, Roan examined his tracks. They led into the creek's cold water and never reappeared on the other side. "Aye, Patch, you be a smart beastie. You been around the mountain a time or two, I'll be betting." Patch had been sighted over these past years by many of the ranchers, but none ever got close enough to kill him.

"Aye, a smart fellow. But why are you now coming so close to me?" If he went after the beast, who would be doing the tracking — him or Patch?

"Nay, beastie," he said, wondering if Patch heard him and if he did, did he recognize the words, comprehend them. "Nay, I'll leave you be for now."

He mounted the dun, rode on toward the Q-C Ranch house and covered the short distance in not more than fifteen minutes.

Ahead of him lay the Q-C compound. Built in the center of a five-mile square of level plain, it lay to the south and east of a thick line of ponderosa pines, planted as a break against raw north winds.

The outbuildings, positioned in a manner convenient to their use, varied in size. Their austere exteriors, although solid and well-kept, told those

18

who saw them they were intended for work, pure and simple.

The main ranch house, no more decorative than the other buildings, was constructed of rough logs chinked with hardened clay. Like a fortress, it stood two imposing stories high. Windows, unadorned by shutters, stared out onto the lesser structures of the compound.

A slender Indian woman answered Roan's knock on the back door. Her dark eyes sparkled when she smiled and greeted him. "Come in, Roan McCrae. Warren told me to expect you today." She laughed, a throaty, lilting sound. "I've near worn out the carpets under all the windows waiting for you."

Roan's laughter joined hers. "Tula Moon, you are, without a doubt, the prettiest woman I know. And you just keep getting prettier, but you sure are full with the blarney. Are you certain you haven't a touch of the Irish?"

She chuckled and clasped his arm as she led him into the large parlor where Warren Quade sat before a blazing fire, a ledger opened in his lap. He snapped the book shut as Roan entered and motioned to a chair opposite him. "Sit down, Roan, if you can get that woman to turn loose of your arm."

Tula Moon hugged it closer. "It's such a strong arm. I wonder if his whole body matches it," she teased.

"By the saints," Roan answered, "I'm certainly willing to let you find out."

She gave him a shove toward the chair. "You would start backtreading before I got the second button on your shirt unfastened."

Roan and Warren both guffawed.

Still smiling, Tula enticed them with, "I baked an apple pie. Would you two like some of it?"

"And coffee, too," Warren replied.

"I know." Tula turned to leave the room, adding over her shoulder, "With just a dash of whiskey."

Roan watched her with an appreciative eye and shook his head. "She's a fine woman, Warren Quade. It's a puzzle why you don't marry her."

"Why should I? Hell, man, she's happy with our arrangement. She doesn't want it any different. Besides," he pointed to a portrait hanging over the mantle. The woman in the picture was lovely, flaxen-haired and gentle looking. "Tula loved Josie as much as I did. She respects her memory."

"Aye, I suppose you're right. It's a sorrow I never knew your wife."

"I've said it before, Roan, you wouldn't have liked her. Josie was an easterner, sophisticated, too delicate for this country. It's what killed her. I wasn't smart enough to realize it until too damned late."

Tula returned with a tray and placed it on a low table between the two men. "I'll leave you to your talk, but —" She patted Roan's stubbled cheek. "You'd better not sneak out of here without telling me goodbye, do you hear?"

20

"I wouldn't think of it, pretty lass. And thank you kindly for the pie."

She smiled and drifted out of the room. Warren reached for one of the coffee cups.

"You know, Roan, I've often wondered why you and Tula Moon get along so well. I think I've finally figured it out."

"Hell, man, there's no great figuring to be done. She's a true beauty, that one."

Quade shook his head. "No, it's more. I have a feeling Tula's a lot like your Katie. Am I right?"

"Aye." Roan's face took on a faraway look. Sadness misted his eyes. "Aye, a lot like Katie."

"Sorry, Roan. I thought you could talk about it by now."

"It's nothing to concern yourself with, Warren Quade. I was just considering what you said."

"About Tula Moon and Katie being alike, you mean?"

"Aye. I hadn't thought of it, but it's true. Me Katie was a rare lass, beautiful and full of love." The room faded into a flurry of memories. Forgotten was the Q-C ranch house. In its place stood the cabin Roan had built of logs and love, small, cozy, filled with the warmth of Katie's smile. In its rooms, she seemed like a bright meadow flower that touched every stick of furniture with her fresh scent.

When the scene changed with a suddenness that drew Roan back to the present, he felt the salt-laden warmth of tears edging onto his cheeks. He lifted his head. His voice hoarse, grief-stricken, he asked, "Why don't they believe me — the townsfolk? Hell, you've only to live here one winter to know how the northers can blow in, sudden like. I was just too far from home when that one hit. I'd have died had I not sought shelter."

"I've always believed you, Roan. You know that."

As though he hadn't heard, Roan continued, "People didn't know me Katie as well as they thought they did. Why, she could shoot as well as meself. I got no idea why she went out to protect them calves with nothing more'n a stick in her hands."

Quade leaned back in his chair and slung his leg over the arm. "I'm about to tell you something, Roan. It's partly why I asked you to stop by. I've never talked about this with anyone except Tula Moon. She's an educated woman, as you know. Reads everything she can get her hands on. Reads damned college books that'd put me clean to sleep in five minutes. Anyway, according to her, after Josie died I had one hell-uva — let me say it right, like she did — one helluva *guilt complex*."

"Why should you feel a guilt over your wife's death. I heard she died from the ague. Are you telling me that ain't true?"

It's true all right. But if I hadn't been such a self-centered bastard. . . ." His voice trailed off into a sigh. Several uncomfortable seconds passed before he spoke again. "You see, I owned this rangeland several years before I married Josie. Went to Chicago one year to buy some registered stock. I met her there. She was a city girl clean through. I knew it, but I didn't think I could live without her and I *knew* I couldn't stand being cooped up in the city. Never mind how she felt."

Roan settled back, popping the last bite of pie into his mouth and washing it down with a gulp of whiskey-laced coffee, now turned cold.

"First couple of years," Quade's voice droned, "she seemed content enough. But then she started getting restless. Wanted to go back to the city — 'Just for a visit' — she said. I was too busy building the ranch up to be taking trips to Chicago. She missed the people, the nice eateries, the theater. We argued a lot. She told me more times than I care to count that she was lonely. I guess it helped a little when she hired Tula Moon. It just wasn't enough."

"Where did she find Tula?" Roan asked.

"Off the Dakota reservation. Tula worked for the Indian agent there. She did everything for Josie, waited on her hand and. . . ." He paused again, obviously drifting in and out of the past. "Josie ran away. Went off to Missoula. Guess she figured any city would do. I was damned angry, but after about three days I went begging for her to come back."

"And she did, so how the devil can you put the blame on yourself?"

Quade, as though he spoke now only to a

23

memory, ignored the question. "I loved her. I told myself she loved me. But you see, I wanted it all — her and this ranch. She cared nothing about the ranch. She didn't belong here."

"And you feel her unhappiness brought on the sickness?"

"Maybe it didn't bring it on, but when she came down sick, I should have sold this place and taken her away so she'd at least have had the will to live. But I didn't. She was ill on and off for more than a year and one day she took to bed for good. Two more days and she died."

Roan pushed himself out of the chair and shuffled to the fireplace, his sight fastened on the dancing flames. Things weren't like that between him and Katie. Katie resembled the land, sort of wild and free. But Quade's words reached deep inside him, wrenching out an understanding. "So your Josie died and you have this guilt driving you. Do you think I have the same guilt over me Katie's dying?"

Quade managed a wan smile and nodded. "Don't you?"

"No. I —"

"Listen, Roan, after Josie died I walked around with an anger no one could stop. I hated the world and everyone in it. Half my crew quit me. If someone mentioned Josie's name, I took them to task — including Tula. One day she'd had enough and she didn't make it easy on me. She said even if I *was* responsible for Josie's death, there was nothing could be done about it now.

I could either forgive myself, try to forget and go on with my life, or I could drive myself crazy, kill myself or, worse yet, kill someone else."

"I think I see what you're driving at. When I go into town, I go looking for trouble. You're telling me it's me guilt causing it, that I'm seeing me own failings and putting them on someone else."

"You deliberately provoke men sometimes, Roan." Quade, feet flat on the floor, leaned forward, resting his arms across his knees. "Last Saturday, you rode into town smelling like something off a gut wagon and you did it on purpose."

"Aye, that I did."

"You could have stopped any of a dozen places and cleaned yourself up."

"And how, friend Quade, would cleaning meself up have been helping me? As it turned out, I ended up in the dirt fighting with the likes of Jake Tanner."

"My God, man, I'm glad Jake Tanner took up the fight with you. You'd have killed Azle Steppe sure as hell."

"Aye." Roan rubbed his hand across his face. "I've given that some thought meself. But you must know I never cared a whit for Azle Steppe."

"Everyone knows that, but before Katie died, you at least *tried* to get along with him."

Roan sat and studied Warren closely. When Roan and Katie settled in this territory six years ago, the few acres of ground they bought had formed the southeast corner of Q-C range.

Quade had always been his friend. "Aye," he said softly, "I tried."

"Tell me, Roan. Two years ago, when you came home and found Katie dead, did you really think maybe you could have made it through that storm?"

Roan's face clouded with anguish. He clenched his fists. "By the saints, I should have tried. Maybe me Katie would still be sharing me bed."

The room was quiet, with only the crackling wood in the fireplace to break the stillness.

Warren Quade's hushed voice interrupted the silence. "Roan, you're being foolish. That norther was one of the worst this territory has had in years. You're as tough a man as comes down the divide, but you wouldn't have lasted an hour. Hell, I lost nine head of cattle that couldn't make it to the breaks."

Roan, his head lowered, said nothing. He simply shook his head and regarded his hands, fingers knit together.

"We're a lot alike, Roan, you and me, but I learned to live with the loss of Josie. You've let your loss turn you into a hard-assed sonofabitch. Think about it, man. Even those wolves that attacked Katie waited until after the storm was done. You told me that yourself. You said you tracked them."

"Aye, fresh tracks right back to their lair."

Abruptly, Warren stood, coffee cup in hand. "Grab your cup," he told Roan. "Let's head for the kitchen. That fool woman's too damn polite to interrupt us. Let's go bother her."

Thankful for the interruption, for relieving him momentarily of the painful burden of Katie's death, Roan followed.

The ranch kitchen was small and compact. Aromas of sweet yeast and bubbling coffee mingled with the warmth from the cookstove. Warren lifted the granite coffee pot off a warmer at the back of the stove.

Tula Moon removed two loaves of bread from the oven. She glanced at the cup in Warren's hand and smiled. "Why didn't you call? I would have brought more."

"We knew you were busy," Warren said, pouring a full cup and seating himself at the table. He motioned for Roan to do the same.

Roan's hands trembled. Tula moved to his side and laid her hand over his, steadying the stream of hot coffee as it arced into the cup. "What does this mean?" she asked, directing the question to Warren. "The solid rock shakes. What have you two been talking about?"

Warren waited until Roan seated himself. "I think I've about convinced Roan to rejoin life."

Tula pulled a bread knife from the drawer and sawed through one of the loaves. "I hadn't noticed Roan had deserted life."

"The men in the Association have felt the none-too-gentle touch of his absence. Jake Tanner, for instance. Besides, woman, it wouldn't matter what he did, you'd find some excuse for him."

"That may be so." She placed a plate of bread on the table beside a bowl of freshly churned butter and a jar of raw honey. "But I recall another man who was much the same after his wife died." She poured herself a cup of coffee and joined them.

"Exactly what I've been telling him."

"Aye," Roan answered quietly and bit into a thick slice of bread.

"Is it good, Roan?" Tula asked.

He nodded vigorously. "Aye, lass, were it not for me friend, Warren Quade here, you'd have to contend with the likes of me. I'd marry you in a minute would you have me."

Tula Moon laughed. "It's good to know. If Warren kicks me out, I promise I'll come running."

Warren grinned and reached for his third slice of bread. "If you wait for her, Roan, I suggest you'll die a lonely old man. You see, along with her other obvious virtues, I couldn't live without her cooking."

"You've never struck me as a fool." God, the light banter was good after the memories had torn him apart inside.

"Will you stay for supper?" Tula asked. "I'll fix something special."

"I'm thanking you, me darling," Roan answered, "but I've a long road to travel tonight."

"Where you headed?" Quade asked.

"Home," Roan said quietly and found that the word covered his wounds with warm balm.

"You're a wise man, Warren Quade. If you can live with your wife's ghost, then I can live with me Katie's and I'll be leaving now." He retrieved his hat and walked outside, accompanied by Warren and Tula.

"What about money, Roan?" Quade asked. "You'll need supplies." He reached into his pocket.

Roan stayed his hand. "It's a fine friend you are. I have enough for me needs, thanks to the Association. But I'll tell you true, the Association can kill its own wolves from now on. I've slain the last for bounty."

"What about the lobo? You giving up on him?"

"I never really went after that one."

"Wasn't he there when Katie was attacked?"

"That he was, but afterwards. His tracks overlayed the others. He only came to investigate. He's no killer and he runs with no pack. Like me, I guess, he's a loner."

He swung into the saddle and shifted his gaze from Warren to Tula and back again. "I'll be thanking the both of you for staying me friends through it all."

He heeled his horse into a lope.

Behind him, Quade said, "He's a good man, Tula, but he's right when he says he's like the wolf — a loner."

"Aye," Tula Moon replied in perfect mimicry of Roan's brogue. "But I don't think he likes it, not really. He isn't a loner, Warren, just a very lonely man."

Roan was almost out of earshot when Tula said, "He'll need us, Warren, and soon. I felt the Devil Ice wash over me just before he left."

Chapter Three

Roan gazed skyward, studying the ring of ice crystals which encircled the full moon. Well past midnight he rode into the weed-infested yard of his ranch.

Halting the dun, he sat loose in the saddle, to survey the area. In the moonlight, he could barely see the white picket fence a hundred or so yards west of the cabin, the fence he erected the day after he buried Katie. He hadn't done it for looks, but because he couldn't stand the sight of the mounded earth that covered the only woman he believed himself capable of loving.

God, that day was as vivid now as it had been then. The thought of her death brought back the desolation, the loneliness, the pain. He snorted. The fence hadn't helped. It only served to remind him what it hid from view. Cold fingers of bitterness clutched at him now. The wind soughed through the trees, the chill racked his body. He waited for the sensation to pass.

He turned the dun and rode closer to the fence. Dismounting, he opened the gate, which protested with a loud screech, and walked to the foot of Katie's grave. Hat in hand, he spoke in soft tones, his voice choked with emotion.

"Katie, me love, 'tis been a long two years. Just this day, me dear friend, Warren Quade, made me realize how wrong me thinking has been. Had I tried to come to you that day, I'd have been laying there beside you and you wouldn't have wanted that. I loved you, me Katie girl. Never will I forget you, but I'm coming home now and, saints be willing, here I'll remain. I'm putting your ghost to rest in me mind. I'll always think of you and the love we shared, but it's living I need to get on with."

He placed his hat on his head and turned away, whispering, "Goodnight, me darling Katie."

As he closed the gate behind him, a low moaning sound assailed his ears. "The wind," he said. The moan slithered through the night air again. But it was *not* the wind, not for all the roses in Ireland. More like the wail of the banshee, mourning, as he did, Katie's death.

He stayed his mount, turned in the saddle and peered into the distance. Not fifty feet away, in a small clearing, sat Patch. Roan studied the lobo. Their eyes met briefly before the animal stretched forward into a relaxed position and laid his head on his forepaws. He emitted another mournful moan.

"You know, don't you, boy?" Roan asked softly. "You know your kind killed me Katie. Somehow, beastie, you're feeling what I'm feeling."

A barely audible whine escaped Patch's throat in answer.

"Did you lose your darling mate, too, me boy? Is that why you prowl this land alone?"

Patch's big head cocked to the side as though he didn't quite understand the words, but wanted to. Rising to a sitting position, the wolf regarded Roan.

"Aye, I'd bet a copper against Finney's pot of gold that's the answer. We're of a common mind, Patch, you and meself." He kicked the horse into an ambling walk. Patch's keen eyes followed him as if he waited for more words.

"All right, me furry friend, I'll tell you something else. I'll not be killing any more of your kind. Will they leave me be, I'll be doing the same."

Patch raised his head. His tongue lolled from one side of his mouth. His bushy tail curled up and over his back. He trotted off, his retreating form dissolving in the lessening moonlight.

"I'll pass me next sop of pure Irish whiskey if he didn't understand every word I said," Roan said and guided the dun toward the cabin.

He stepped onto the porch he had built with such care across the entire front of the log structure. His hand trembled as he reached for the door. Two years, two long, miserable years, it had been since he set foot inside the home he constructed for Katie and him. Each day that passed made this moment more difficult, but he promised Warren Quade and, in a way, Katie.

He shoved on the door. A loud "scre-e-e" from the untended hinges answered his thrust.

Someone — maybe him — had pulled the heavy linen drapes which framed the windows. The moonlight sent a needle-thin shaft of light through the tiny separation between the two halves. Aside from that, the room was dark as the pitch Roan had spread on the sloped roof to keep out the rain.

No matter. Even in the dark, he knew every board, every peg of the cabin. He had placed each with love for his new bride. His own footsteps thumped across the once polished floor, now gritty with dust as Roan hurried toward the stone mantle above the fireplace. Once the lamp was lit, perhaps the shadows inside him would abate.

In the flickering light, he studied the room, untouched these two years. The settee in front of the fireplace and the matching chair at one end had been a project over which he and Katie had laughed, and argued, and laughed again. He designed the pair and spent hours cutting and smoothing the wood. Katie spent the same hours at the spinning wheel and loom, fashioning the colorful cushions on which they rested together before a dancing fire.

Tanned hide rugs dotted the floors in both parlor and bedroom, where he wandered now, realizing he had entered the room where he and Katie had consummated their love. He stared at the huge four-poster bed dominating the room. Katie had brought it all the way from Ireland with her. The coverlet was a part of her dowry, stitched by her own fingers with great care. Surrounded by soft green velvet was a snow white swan, as pure and beautiful as Katie herself. He ran his fingers across the smooth fabric. Suddenly, she seemed so close he smelled the faint scent of the lilac water which always lingered in the thick strands of her auburn hair.

Roan became aware for the first time of the salty tears coursing their way down his leathered cheeks. Weary and sad, he yielded to his grief, threw himself across the bed and wept.

Roan awakened with bright sunshine warming his face, despite the chill throughout the cabin's three small rooms. He arose and stoked the hot coals in the fireplace. In the kitchen, he started a fire in the cookstove, ran a handful of beans through the coffee grinder and threw the result into a pot of cold water, setting it on a back burner to boil.

He sauntered through the rear door onto a small stoop he'd built for Katie so she could cool herself from her labors and feast her eyes on the wildly beautiful rangeland spreading out before her.

The sunshine warmed the early October crispness. Winter would soon roar down from the mountains. With luck, Roan would have a few weeks before it devastated the land. There was much to be done, all the work he should have completed during the long months he'd been gone.

He gazed into the distance. Somewhere out there, on unfenced Q-C and Double S range, he had a couple dozen head of Herefords and a matched pair of wagon-broke horses he would have to round up. Following that, he needed to ride to the nearest Q-C line camp and purchase enough feed to last through the winter.

As far as he was concerned, he wouldn't starve, thanks to Quade's generosity. Plenty of meat hung in the smokehouse and he had fresh eggs daily. He sighed. If the varmints hadn't gotten to the hens, they would have survived on the wild oats and Indian corn.

As if assuring Roan, a cock crowed from the direction of the henhouse. He smiled. If the rooster was alive, so were the hens. Five years now, he had owned that big gamecock. How well he remembered some three years ago when he and Katie watched a weasel barely escape with its life. Bleeding profusely from punctures caused by the cock's long spurs, the weasel fled, squealing as Roan and Katie laughed at the sight.

"I'll not be worrying about me prized hens," Katie vowed, "not after seeing that."

Sliding Katie's memory back into its corner of his mind, he returned to the kitchen and downed a sturdy breakfast of steak and eggs washed down with black coffee.

Afterward, he saddled the dun and rode off through the tall pines toward a clearing. There, he found his cattle along with eight calves and the horses. He swung his mount wide, lessening the width of the circles he made around the herd until they were bunched and ready to drive toward home.

"Hold up, McCrae!" someone shouted.

Roan turned in his saddle and waited as three men rode toward him. It wasn't hard to recognize Jake Tanner. With him were two Double S hands. Roan halted the dun and waited.

Tanner slid his mount to a stop a few feet away. "What the hell you doing on Double S range?" he demanded.

Roan's answer came slow and easy. "Moving me cattle to me own land. Have you some problem with that, Mister Tanner?"

Jake nudged his mount a few steps closer. "They been here near all summer. Been thinking I ought to run them in with the Double S stock — just to see if you got the guts to come get them."

"Aye, I would've done just that," Roan said, his voice low. One of the ranch hands snickered. Tanner gave him a hard look and ordered, "Shut up!" Turning back, he pointed a finger at Roan. "You'd have paid for the grass your mangy animals ate. I promise you that."

"Aye, I would've, and I will now. 'Tis eight calves I have, Jake Tanner. Take three of them."

"How about we take all eight?" Tanner's derisive tone filled the air with malice.

Roan shook his head. "You'll take only three. That's fair enough pay for the rangeland, so small is me herd."

Tanner barked orders to his men. "Get in there and separate them calves — all eight of them."

The two hesitated, looking first at Roan then at Tanner.

Again, Roan shook his head. "Three is me offer. And a fair one, it is."

"You heard what I said, Early," Tanner sneered. "Get in there and get them."

"Aw hell, Jake," Early replied. "Let it go. Double S don't need them calves. McCrae there does. Besides, I think the man's had enough trouble for a while."

Tanner edged his horse nearer to Early's. "You been ordered. You do what I say or you find work somewheres else."

Early's face reddened. "Kiss my butt, *Mister* Tanner. I been wondering anyhow if Q-C needed a good hand." He whirled his mount and galloped away.

With a shocked expression, Tanner turned toward the remaining rider. Before he could renew his demand, the second man shook his head. "I reckon I feel the same way, Jake." With a mock salute, he, too, rode toward the Q-C line. He called over his shoulder, "So long, Roan."

"So long, Eben," Roan replied. "May the sun be warm on your back."

Tanner spun around and pointed a long finger at Roan. "Get them damn cows off Double S range and do it now. Don't let me see them on it again."

He called to the two men, "Early! Eben! You two hold up a damn minute!" He jerked the reins and jabbed his spurs into his horse's flanks.

Roan smiled, peering after the retreating riders. It felt good to have someone on his side for a change, but he'd be willing to bet the two hands would still be taking orders from the likes of Jake Tanner come spring.

For two weeks, Roan worked from first light until darkness halted his labors. Repairing two years of neglect was no small chore.

He mended fence where possible, rebuilt where not. Driftwood had clogged the mountain stream that ran along the east boundary line. Despite scratches from thorny branches and a few too many insect bites, he cleared the brush.

Three long days were spent hauling hay from the nearest Q-C line shack ten miles distant. Not a long ride, but a lonely one with too much time for memories to surface.

He enjoyed his labors. Chopping wood to stock the shed was something he had always loved. His nostrils filled with the scent of sweet resin and his muscles hardened with each cut of the axe. Chips flying into the air, catching prisms of sunlight on droplets of sap was a sight a man could savor.

When the shed was filled to near bulging, Roan sank the axe blade deep into the woodblock and stepped back, smiling, to survey his accomplishment. The next months would be difficult, given the blustering storms which beset the area, but he was nearly ready.

A ride into Buckhorn for supplies completed his tasks and none too soon. As he unhitched the team from the wagon that evening, the gray sky spit its first snowflakes. Winter entered lazily, but would grow into maturity with a swiftness that had caught many men unaware.

Within two weeks, enough snow had fallen to form drifts as deep as fifteen feet. After that, it eased, but Roan wasn't fooled. Snowfall would return with a fury that would turn the first bluster into nothing more than an enjoyable cold spell.

During that break Roan saw Patch again. He sat in the yard fronting the cabin and stared through the window.

On impulse, Roan slipped into his heavy coat and headed for the kitchen. Katie had insisted he build a storage room for their meat, a place where it would keep through summer and winter. He had obliged her by digging a root cellar that was cool year round. He selected a thick steak.

Returning to the front door, he opened it slowly, afraid he would startle the wolf and he would run. But Patch remained where he was, eyeing the steak. He flicked his tongue quickly over his mouth and whined.

Roan tossed the meat toward him. It arced and headed landward. Patch lunged forward, catching the steak in midair, then looked at Roan.

"You're welcome enough, me friend."

The wolf trotted out of the yard and into the open field beyond.

"Come back and share me dinner any time you like."

Again Patch stopped and turned. Roan's glance locked with the wolf's for a moment before the beast curled his tail over his back and lurched across packed snow toward the forest beyond.

Twice more in as many weeks, the wolf returned. Each visit Roan rewarded Patch with a steak feast. On the last of the two visits, Roan opened the door wide and held the steak in his hand.

"Would you like to come inside, me friend, and warm yourself beside the hearth?" he asked.

Patch's neckhairs bristled. From his throat came a low growl.

"Aye, me boy, it's understanding I am. You have a place of your own where you feel safe and it's not in the cabin of a grieving mick."

Thereafter, winter storms raged continuously. The land lay buried beneath a fortress of snow and ice.

Roan's herd fared well, despite the hard winter. A week into the new year, the worst storm of the season hit and remained. He struggled through the blinding white to move two of the suckling calves and their mothers into the barn. The rest huddled in a stand of tall pines at the south break of a thousand-foot peak.

For the next ten days, he arose in the morning, hitched his team to a sled and hauled hay to the weary, snowbound cattle.

"Saints be praised," he whispered, "for seeing me stock through this harsh time. You'll be looking after this tiny piece of earth and it's puzzled I am why you'd bother."

Each evening, he followed the tracks of the

herd to the creek and broke ice so they could drink.

As suddenly as the storm had roared over the land, a chinook whooshed through, melting most of the snow. The stock began to regain their strength.

"I'll be thanking you again, me guardian saints," he said. "You've broken the back of the winter and brought me some peace of mind."

Patch came during that time and returned to his private place with another steak.

When winter refused to relinquish her hold on the land and still another storm roared through, Roan didn't worry as he had before. His beasts, including the wolf, had survived the worst. The rest could be taken in stride.

The warming came haltingly, but it came. The creek ran bank full as mountains sent down their winter coats, to melt into clear, fresh water. Here and there, the barren soil burst forth with greening grass and meadow flowers of every color displayed their glory.

He gazed out over forty acres of treeless ground where he had taken such pride in his stands of hay. In the corner of the field nearest the house had been Katie's pride — her garden. "There's beans and corn aplenty to see us through the bad days," she'd say, jabbing the hoe at another of the stray weeds that had now choked the untended land. "It's not hungry we'll go, Roan McCrae."

He considered reseeding the hay crop. The

thought of aching muscles from clearing the field with a hand scythe brought a sigh from his lips, but he bolstered himself remembering the joy of the harvest as he again swung the scythe, loosing the scent of sweet hay into the air. He never failed to get at least two good cuttings from the ground and smiled as he thought of the loft bulging with the rich feed. The fact that he had prepared well to buy the expensive seed brought still another smile.

With his meager herd, he could never afford to buy such seed, but he had spent the long winter trapping. Two piles of cured pelts lined the wall in the cabin's parlor, more than enough for the seed as well as supplies for the larder.

With his bundles of skins strapped across one of the wagon horses and five of the yearling calves tied along a rope behind, he headed for town. Two of the remaining calves were heifers he would keep to increase his herd. The third was steaks on the hoof.

An hour after he arrived in Buckhorn, he pocketed two hundred twenty-five dollars and his thoughts turned to home. Only the rumbling complaints from his empty stomach kept him from heading back immediately.

He considered the two dining halls in the town — one in the square next to the Last Chance Saloon, the other in the hotel at the far west end. He chose the latter. Too fine a day, it was to head for certain trouble. It wasn't likely he'd meet anyone he knew at the hotel.

Not likely, true, but a premonition of trouble followed him down the street.

Chapter Four

The hotel lobby was, as usual, quiet and sparsely attended. One man, his dungarees faded and patched, signed the register at the desk. The swiftness with which the fellow scribbled on the page proffered by the desk clerk said he'd placed there nothing more than an "X."

The desk clerk frowned. The expression changed to one of disgust as he dropped the room key into the guest's hand. The gesture implied that to touch the poor, ignorant farmer in any way would contaminate the clerk.

Roan shook his head and turned toward the dining room. He could remember when only the wealthy drove up to the door of this building, alighting from their fine carriages, outfitted in the trappings of the rich. Now, it had become a haven for derelicts. He smiled and added with a touch of wistfulness — people like he had been for the past years.

The dining room, like the lobby, was virtually empty. Only a few people sat at the round tables placed randomly throughout the room. At the larger table in the center were several members of the Cattlemen's Association, Warren Quade and Azle Steppe among them.

Roan swung around sharply, prepared to go elsewhere, and hoped no one had spotted him. He retreated only three steps before Warren Quade's voice called his name.

Forcing a smile, he sighed and made a slow turn to face his friend.

Quade signaled with a wave of his hand to come on over. Reluctantly, Roan strode toward the table and stopped a few feet away. He nodded in response to greetings from four of the men. Azle Steppe ignored him.

"I gather you were coming in for supper, Roan," Quade said. "Why don't you join us?" He indicated an empty chair next to him.

"I thank you for your invitation, Warren Quade, but I'll be taking meself to the corner over there." He motioned toward a table set apart from the others.

Quade's expression indicated he understood, but his words were insistent. "Sit down, Roan. We've got us a couple of arguments going here and I think you can straighten out at least one of them."

With a shrug, Roan pulled the chair away from the table and seated himself. A waitress in a uniform that had once been starched and new placed a glass of water and eating utensils wrapped in a napkin in front of him.

"Somebody start passing that food there," Quade ordered. The other men complied, all except Steppe, who pretended not to see the platters and bowls held toward him on their journey around the table.

Roan reached in front of him to grasp the still-steaming rice, gravy, roast and vegetables.

Conversation lagged as the men ate. Quade

broke the clatter of knives and forks when he said, "Roan, we were talking about the wolf problem this winter. Do you still contend your lobo's a loner, not leading a pack?"

"Aye. Even more so now."

"How's that?"

"I've been close to the old boy, not more than fifteen or twenty feet. I've even talked to him."

He ignored the sudden sputtering from Azle Steppe which ended in a coughing fit. Steppe's face reddened when his outburst met first with snickers followed by boisterous laughter.

Roan lowered his head and concentrated on his food.

Steppe wiped his mouth with a napkin, brushed tears from his eyes and choked out, "You actually talk to wild animals, McCrae?"

Without changing expression, Roan answered, "Aye, I find beasties a helluva lot more interesting than people sometimes, Mr. Steppe."

More laughter wound its way around the table, and subsided as Roan's steady gaze fastened on Steppe.

Steppe glared back with naked hatred in his eyes.

"As a matter of truth, Mr. Steppe, it's me feeling that the wolf's lived amongst people rather than with his own kind."

"Is it now?" Steppe sneered.

"Aye, I'm thinking he's been reared that way since he was a pup." Roan shrugged. "Could be the man died or moved on. Who knows? But the fact is, gentlemen, the beast's not afraid of me."

47

"Well, he better damn sure be afraid of me," Steppe snapped. "Me and my boys are going wolf hunting tomorrow and wherever we find that sonofabitch, he's dead."

"What you do with your time and your men, Mr. Steppe, is your business." Roan's voice was firm. "Just don't be looking on me own land."

"Hah! Yours is the first we're coming to!"

Warren Quade brought his fist down on the table top. "All right now. Dammit, Azle, I invited Roan to sit with us because of his knowledge about the wolf. Why don't you listen to him for a change instead of antagonizing him. Damn! You might learn something from him."

At first startled with the outburst from Quade, Steppe's expression turned to dark anger. He jumped to his feet and sent the chair toppling over behind him, crashing to the wooden floor. "Learn something from that dirty mick? Not likely."

"I'll not have this meeting turn into another brawl," Quade said.

Fury blazed in Steppe's eyes. "That's the trouble with this association. Everything is your way, Quade. Well, I've had enough of you! All of you!" He jerked the napkin from its mooring beneath his chin and slung it onto the table. "Now you listen good. On the other matter we talked about. My offer stands and you'll take it or else."

Roan raised his eyebrows in a question aimed at Warren.

48

Quade opened his mouth to speak, but Steppe never gave him the chance. He stabbed a meaty finger in Roan's face. "As for you, the only offer you'll get is my promise to take that piss-assed few acres of yours at my price. You'll take it, you understand that? You'll take it or we'll run you over."

He whirled and stomped from the room, leaving behind half-puzzled, half-amused expressions on the faces of the men at the table.

"Would one of you gentlemen kindly be telling me what the man's speaking of?" Roan asked, drawing their attention back to the food. "What is this offer he's making me for me land?"

"Just that, Roan," Quade answered. "He's made all of us an offer. I was the first. I told him then I wasn't interested. He went to Doc Mason there next." He indicated the tall, stately man seated across the table, a man Roan had seen many times, but only now learned his name.

"And your rangeland, Mr. Mason, Warren Quade tells me borders the Blackfoot reservation." Roan glanced around the table. "But why would Azle Steppe be wanting all your land . . . as well as me own?"

"He wants to squeeze us out," Doc told him. "If he could get my spread, he'd have both ends of what he wants and he'd have a way to squeeze until the rest of you agreed."

Quade added, "It would take a lot of patience to do such a thing and I don't think Azle has that kind of patience."

49

"Faith," Roan said, shaking his head, "what turned the man's thinking this way?"

Quade shrugged. "Who knows? He told us he was bringing in a bigger herd next month and he needed more space." Quade's expression turned more serious. "You watch him, Roan. He's got no great love for you. He might use that wolf to get to you."

"Aye. I've noted he had no great love for the likes of me, but then you might have guessed he's not one of me favorites neither."

The following morning, with breakfast under his belt, Roan reached for his hat and headed for the door. His day was planned and his heart felt light, almost giddy, with the anticipation of re-seeding the forty acres.

The sound of approaching horses drew him to the door. He counted five riders, their horses lined abreast, heading straight for his cabin. He recognized four of them — Azle Steppe, Jake Tanner, and two other hands.

The fifth man was a black man, his skin the color of coal dust. Dressed in traditional range clothes except for a black leather vest closed in front by a single rawhide string, he wore his hat pulled low over his eyes. Only his tight-lipped mouth and determined jaw showed from beneath the shadow of the brim.

A pair of matched Colt revolvers swung in their holsters strapped low on his hips and tied down.

"So," Roan said, "it wasn't a bluff Mr. Azle

50

Steppe was trying on me. It's a range war he'll be wanting."

"Come out here, McCrae," Steppe shouted as the horses stopped just a few feet from the porch.

Roan lifted his rifle from the rack beside the door and leaned it against the wall within easy reach. Belying the quickening of his pulse, he leaned casually against the doorsill. "State your business, Azle Steppe. Me work stands waiting."

With a derisive grunt, Steppe sneered. "Any work you think you got to do today or any time soon's going to be wasted. I'm here to offer five hundred dollars for your deed. Take it or I'll bury you here and now."

He pulled a roll of bills from his jacket pocket and thrust them toward Roan, who remained in position.

Steppe gestured with the bills. "Take it! I won't say it again."

"Aye, and I won't be saying again to get your men off me property."

The stranger gave a low, humorless laugh. "He's got guts. I'll say that for him."

"He's stupid is the word," Steppe answered. "By the way, McCrae, just to show you I mean business, I guess you should meet my new hand." He jerked his thumb toward the black man. "This here's Thax Hilton. Maybe you've heard of him."

Roan tried to mask the jolting surprise when he heard Hilton's name. He knew he'd failed when smiles spread across the faces of Steppe and Tanner. No one in the country had been so hidden from the rest of the world they hadn't heard of Thaxter Ward Hilton. His guns — and fine ones they were — and his expertise in handling them were for hire to anyone who could meet his price. He wasn't cheap.

"Aye, I've heard of him. What is it you're intending, Azle Steppe? Is it all-out war you're wanting?"

"Nobody wants to listen. I need range."

"And me piss-assed few acres as you kindly called them is the range you're needing?"

Steppe shook his head. "You're nothing more than a nuisance, a speck of lint on my plan. I want you out of here."

Roan considered his words. "Is it your thinking that buying killers like this one will serve your purpose?" He shook his head. "All you'll be doing is spilling blood."

For the first time, Hilton thumbed the brim of his hat upward revealing piercing black eyes, their whites a startling contrast to his dark skin. "You have a big mouth, Mr. McCrae," he said in a deep, resonant voice, his words perfectly enunciated. "As I said, you show courage, but hear this. I have never spilled blood as you put it except in a stand-up fight."

Jake Tanner laughed. "Show this stinking wolfer how you do it, Thax."

Hilton fixed Tanner with an arrogant gaze. "Only my friends call me Thax," he said, his voice cold.

Tanner, openly angered, held his words in check.

Roan smiled. Even the bullying Jake Tanner was afraid of this broad-shouldered, slim-hipped black man.

Turning back to Azle Steppe, Hilton waited for orders. Steppe's slight nod was enough. Hilton slid easily from the saddle. His left foot still in the stirrup, one hand wrapped around the saddlehorn, he stopped at the snap of a rifle bolt. He remained motionless, regarding the barrel of Roan's rifle, cocked and pointed at his midsection.

"That's far enough, Mister Hilton," Roan warned. "If you value your belly, you'll not be moving a muscle." With the rifle barrel, he pushed the screen door open and moved onto the porch. "Azle Steppe, it's your decision. But if it's me advice you'll be taking, I'd say it would be wise to stay very still or Mr. Hilton here will be taking the first shot and yourself the second." He looked into each man's face in turn, keeping his expression one of promise. "Would any of you be wanting to test me words?"

Hilton made an effort to lift himself back into the saddle.

Roan's finger tightened on the trigger. "Stay, Mr. Hilton."

Hilton relaxed as he was, his position hardly one for a gunfighter. Fingers flexing, one hand moved slowly toward the right-hand revolver.

Roan gestured with the rifle. "Tell me, Thaxter Hilton, do you truly believe you could draw the gun faster than me finger could pull this trigger?"

53

Hilton's narrowed eyes studied Roan before he answered, "They tell me I'm fast, McCrae." He shook his head. "I'm not that fast."

"Are you comfortable there, Mr. Hilton?" Roan asked, deliberately prolonging the moment, knowing full well the unwieldy position was cramping the gunman's muscles.

Hilton didn't answer.

"And am I understanding you aren't interested in testing who's the fastest?"

"I'm no gambler," Hilton said. "Especially not with my life and against a stacked deck. No, McCrae, I have no intention of testing something I know I can't win."

Hilton, his leg still caught in the stirrup, made an effort to hide his discomfort. The leg muscle began a spasmodic jerk. He tightened the muscles which rippled beneath his dungarees. The effort did little toward controlling the spasms.

"Now, Mr. Hilton," Roan said, "you and me, we got no reason to be killing each other. I'm thinking the wise thing for meself to do right now is to shoot you and save me rancher friends a lot of grief."

"Do it then," Hilton goaded.

"I'm no murderer, but I'm thinking if you continue to hang around with the likes of Little Caesar there," he indicated Azle Steppe, "you'll be buzzard bait soon enough." He raised the rifle barrel until it was level with Hilton's head. "You keep them hands of yours where I can see them and climb back on your horse."

Hilton nodded and lifted himself into the saddle.

Roan turned the rifle toward Steppe. "Now get off me property."

Steppe hesitated a moment too long. Roan squeezed back on the trigger. With a deafening blast, the shot sent Steppe's hat sailing from his head.

Steppe yanked his horse around. "You're dead, you mick sonofabitch," he said. Jabbing hard with his spurs, he sped off in a cloud of dust. Tanner and the other two hands followed.

Only Thax Hilton remained with one hand gripping the saddlehorn, the other holding tight rein on his startled mount.

Roan aimed the rifle in his direction. "I meant yourself as well, Mr. Hilton. I'll thank you to be leaving now."

Hilton calmed his mount by patting him on the shoulder. "I'm not ready to leave just yet, McCrae," he said. His eyes held their gaze with Roan's. "You made a fool of me today. I don't like to look foolish."

"Is that a fact, Mr. Hilton? It's truly sorry I am."

"It won't happen again." The words, uttered softly, carried a loud threat.

Roan nodded. "Aye. You're right. It won't happen again. Next time I see you and the likes of them others on me property, I'll shoot you and wonder if it was right later."

"You're no killer, McCrae. But I am. Not a

murderer, mind you. You were right about that, but I have no qualms about killing a man in a gunfight."

"I've no doubt about your abilities, but I'm doubting you'd shoot an unarmed man or wait in ambush. It would take no second thought for Azle Steppe to do either."

"I work for wages," Hilton said, his eyes never wavering in their steady gaze. "Steppe pays well for my services. He wants a lot of people taken out of his way. You were the first."

"But you made a big mistake, Mr. Hilton. If you stick with Azle Steppe, you'll wind up in jail or dead. He's a hungry man, Steppe is. Power hungry."

With a curt nod, Hilton said, "That's what usually starts range wars — someone like Steppe who's wealthy and wants to be wealthier. He wants it all. Like most, he believes if he shows enough force, people will fold and let him have what he wants. He's a stupid man. And I despise stupidity."

"Then why do you work for him?"

"I told you why — money. Look, men like me —" He hesitated and Roan thought he saw a flash of anger in the dark eyes. "What I mean is, I used to work for wages, when I could find someone that would hire a black man. I'm an educated man, McCrae. I'm not shoveling manure or cleaning outhouses for anyone."

Roan waited for him to finish.

"Even risked my life for a while for forty and

56

found. Then I learned I was faster than the average gunnie."

"Aye, but it's still risking your life you are."

"Not until today. I made a mistake today, but I'll remember. You're a lot smarter than Azle Steppe. When we meet again, I won't take you for granted. I've been paid to kill you. I'll earn my pay. Count on it."

"But you'll not be doing such today."

"The day isn't over yet."

He turned his mount and galloped after the others, calling over his shoulder, "You better watch out after that pet wolf of yours, McCrae. Steppe wants him dead, too."

Chapter Five

With nerves strung gut tight, Roan loaded his seed onto one of the wagon horses and led it toward the field. He'd thought of remaining in the cabin, of waiting for Hilton's threatening words — "The day's not over yet" — to materialize, but what good would it do? If they met again, it was just as well out here in the open.

His muscles relaxed in response to the backbreaking work of seeding the acreage by hand. A quick glance skyward told him he had maybe an hour of daylight left. He hurried his pace.

In the near distance, he heard cattle bawling and men shouting. The Double S boundary lay to the southeast a mile or so. He tuned his ears to the sounds. Sometimes they traveled easily in the evening stillness. If they were working near the line . . .

But the noise grew in intensity and his awareness heightened. They were stampeding the cattle toward his spread.

He dropped the seed sack and ran. His rifle leaned against a tree trunk at the edge of the field. His horse was staked out nearby, but he made a quick decision not to ride in. It was a half mile to the cabin. He would easily be seen on the big wagon horse. Before they spotted him, he wanted to know what they intended. Afoot and running hard, he headed toward the wooded area.

The panicked herd drew closer. A hundred yards or so from the cabin, Roan crawled behind a clump of berry bushes and peered through the bare limbs just as bawling cattle rumbled into the yard.

Behind the cows, he counted eight Double S riders, including Jake Tanner. They circled the cabin twice before Thax Hilton walked out through the front door.

"He's not here," Hilton shouted, working his way through the cattle, now beginning to calm and mill around. "I'll check the barn for his horse."

Tanner raised himself in his stirrups and yelled to the men, "You two, circle the barn when Hilton goes in. The rest of you get some of that dry grass. I want this place burning good before we leave."

Roan shouldered the rifle and aimed toward Tanner's broad chest. "You dirty —" His anger was strong, but his common sense was stronger. Before his finger tightened on the trigger, the thought struck him that he'd surely die if he let the riders know of his presence. He might take Jake Tanner to hell with him, but he had to consider the worth of such a plan. He relaxed his grip on the gun and laid it on the ground.

His hands balled into fists as he watched flames lick the walls of his cabin. Anger subsided into the sharp pain of sadness as he remembered the joyous days he spent with Katie inside those walls. His emotions switched again when he caught sight of several head of cattle munching grass near Katie's grave.

He parted the limbs to give him clear vision in that direction. The picket fence stood, unharmed. He sighed in relief. "You can thank the lucky stars above you, Jake Tanner," he whispered. Had the fence been down and Katie's grave desecrated, nothing but his own death would have kept him from emptying the rifle into the Double S crew.

Thax Hilton's voice drew his attention away from the gravesite. "He's not in the barn," Hilton called. "His saddle horse is gone. Maybe he headed for town."

"And maybe he didn't," Tanner answered. "Maybe he's out trying to protect that damned wolf since he knows we're after it."

Tanner split the air with a shrill whistle and shouted, "Come on. This cabin's burning good. Let's find that wolf."

Tanner made one more circle around the cabin.

Thax Hilton guided his mount through the cattle and halted within a few feet of Roan's hiding place. His voice was low, but firm. "Sorry about your home, McCrae. It was that or your life. Go easy."

Hilton spurred the horse and headed after Tanner who led the group northwest toward the divide.

Roan lifted himself and peered over the bushes toward the diminishing forms. His brows furrowed in astonishment. "Saints be thanked," he murmured. "The man knew where I be all along. 'Tis a strange game he plays."

A bitter smile twitched the corners of his mouth as his uneasiness lessened. Those wild screaming banshees from the Double S could never get close enough to kill Patch. He let the thought drift around in his mind. At first the words had been meant to bolster hope. In the end, they had become fact.

Patch was too smart for them.

Roan's emotions roiled as the blaze consumed the cabin he and Katie had worked so hard to build. Turning away from the hungry flames, he walked, more bone weary than he'd ever been, toward the picket fence and Katie's grave.

He half-heartedly shooed the cows munching the lush grass around the fenced site. In the fast-approaching darkness, he was suddenly overcome with devastating loneliness.

He leaned against the gate and stared at the headstone. His eyes brimmed with tears. He could hear Katie's words the evening he had pronounced the cabin completed. Hand in hand, they walked through the three comfortable rooms and Katie said, " 'Tis a good thing you've accomplished, Roan McCrae, and for now, 'tis room enough." Her arm slid around his waist. She pressed closer to him and added, "But next year, it'll be another room we'll have to add — for the children, you know."

That night, she conceived, but three months later . . . Roan looked at the small marker next to Katie's, nothing more than a crude board with an angel and a date burned into its surface. No name. They hadn't had time to choose one for the son Roan had always dreamed of having.

He sighed. In their short marriage, the death of the tiny boy had been the only blight — that and the fact that Katie never again conceived.

Startled out of his memories, he spun toward an almost imperceptible sound — like a muffled bark.

Again, the strange sound drifted on the breeze. He scanned the area around him.

Patch sat a few feet away, his head turning first to the burning cabin then back to Roan as though asking, "What happened here?"

" 'Tis a scurvy lot they are, them that works for the Double S," Roan told him.

The wolf cocked his head, his eyes now fixed on Roan.

"They be wanting us, Patch, you and meself."

The wolf's pointed ears flicked and returned to their attentive stiffness.

"Aye, me friend. 'Tis best we head far to the north where you'll be safe — meself as well." He snapped his fingers and said, "Come." The wolf fell in behind him, still more proof the beast had been raised by man.

A scant half hour later, Roan sat the dun and watched the roof of the cabin fall in a shower of orange sparks.

Patch whined, drawing Roan's attention. The wolf sat, as he had for the last several minutes, not ten feet away, his eyes riveted on the burning remains of Roan's memories. Did he really see sadness in Patch's eyes? Was it truly possible the great beast could feel his own grief?

He nudged the dun and yanked on the lead rope of one of the wagon horses that carried feed, a packet of jerked beef and a half dozen smoked steaks. The only thing available for a bedroll was a tarp which he rolled and tied to the animal's pack. In addition, he had found a battered old tin pan which would do for cooking over a campfire until he could get something better.

He glanced down at Patch. "We'll hie us toward Saskatchewan, old son, where it's safe enough you'll be. Then I'm coming back. Azle Steppe and his scurvy crew will pay for this. I'll swear that to you, boy, by all that's holy."

Wanting to turn and run back to the gravesite and weep with Katie, Roan spurred his mount, galloped out of the yard and never looked back.

Beneath his breath, he cursed Jake Tanner, then said aloud to Patch, "Tanner and his henchmen headed northwest, Patch, me boy, so 'tis safer for you and meself if we move the opposite. You'll be agreeing to that, I'd reckon." He pointed toward the Q-C and Dakota boundary. Patch bounded forward, his tail curled over his back. A few yards distant, he turned and waited to make certain Roan followed.

If the stars could be believed, it was close to

an hour past midnight, safe enough to make camp. They were at least ten miles west of Warren Quade's ranch house. For a certainty, Tanner would return to the Double S that night. He might even swing around to the west of the Q-C. Should that be the case, there must be no fire to pinpoint his position.

He grained the horses and staked them in a grassy area. From the food packet, he took a steak and gave it to Patch. For himself he chose a strip of jerked beef. He, too, would have liked one of the steaks, but he preferred his at least introduced to the embers of a campfire. Besides, all he needed was something to still the rumbling of his belly and jerked beef would do that just as well.

He leaned against a nearby boulder and contemplated the night sky and his situation. One hell of a mess he'd gotten himself into, it appeared. For two long years he had wandered around, caring not a whit for anything or anybody. Then, after his talk with Quade, he had finally seen his life as it was, lost and aimless.

Come spring, he would have worked harder than ever to build his small farm into what he and Katie had dreamed of. Not an empire — it could never be that — but comfortable. He'd even given thought, in moments of extreme loneliness, to finding another woman like his Katie, if that indeed was possible.

He sighed and shook his head. All those thoughts were wasted now.

Damn Azle Steppe!

But there would be time later to find a way to repay Steppe's greed. Now he had to get Patch to a safe haven.

He rolled into his tarp and slept, his dreams sprinkled with hungry flames and dancing sparks and . . . Katie's voice, grieving over the white swan coverlet. Then the swan rose from the flames and flew toward Roan. The bird alighted on a moonlit path a few feet in front of him.

But what he saw on the pathway wasn't a swan. It was his friend, Patch, his gray-green eyes pleading for help.

The sun indicated mid-morning when Roan rode out of a long, narrow ravine. He reached level ground just as Tanner and the Double S crew emerged from a wooded area too nearby for Roan to turn back into the ravine undetected.

He cursed himself for believing Tanner would take the men back to the ranch last night. Tanner followed orders — Azle Steppe's orders — and those orders were to get Roan and the wolf.

He surveyed the situation. A few hundred yards in front of him was a thick stand of timber. He heeled the dun and jerked the pack horse's lead rope. He had something close to a snowball's chance in a forest fire of outrunning the Double S men, but the protective cover of the woods might improve his and Patch's odds for staying alive.

He purchased the edge of the pine woods and wound his way through dense trees. Certain he had reached safety, he dismounted and tied the horses securely.

Patch stood a few feet away watching. Roan turned to him, pointing to the ground near the horses. "Here, me friend. Stay!"

Obediently, the wolf ambled to the spot he indicated and sank back on his haunches, his eyes drinking in Roan's every movement.

" 'Tis a fight they be wanting, me boy, and 'tis a fight they'll get." He lifted the rifle from the saddle boot and ran back to the forest's edge.

Tanner and the men, now less than fifty yards away pounded toward him. Tanner's big hand wrapped tightly around his rifle. He used the gun to gesture for the crew to ride faster.

Roan leaned against a young pine and waited until the riders covered half the distance. Telling himself, Now! he cocked and fired. The shot found its mark. The rifle flew out of Tanner's hand.

"Sonofabitch!" Tanner shouted. He yanked his horse to a halt and motioned the others to do likewise.

"Stay your ground, Jake Tanner," Roan called.

Tanner's laugh, mocking, echoed across the distance. "Come out of there, McCrae. We want the wolf. We know he's with you. We've seen him."

"Aye," Roan answered. "I never denied he was with me. And you don't just want the likes of

Patch, you want the both of us."

"What if I do?"

"You'll rot in hell before you get us. Might be one of your men or Mr. Hilton there will kill us, but not yourself, Jake Tanner. The next shot I fire will be the last you hear. I'll see the bullet splits your black heart."

Thax Hilton, sitting his mount noticeably apart from the others, thumbed his hat back on his head and laughed. "Why didn't you do that when you fired that first shot, McCrae? You had the perfect chance."

"Shut up, Hilton!" Tanner spat the words. "Damn you, you're daring that stupid mick to kill me."

Hilton glanced at Tanner, eyes narrowed to slits. He pointed his finger and said between clenched teeth, "Don't *ever* tell me to shut up, and don't ever call the man a mick again."

"You got a problem with that, Hilton?"

"I don't have problems. I make problems. If you'd call him a mick, you'd have no qualms about calling me a nigger and I wouldn't like that. You're like a catfish. Big mouth and no brains. I don't like you much, Tanner, and I generally do away with things I don't like. Do we understand each other?"

The silence after he spoke was ominous and filled with threat.

"Hell," Tanner said, "forget it. Just do what you been paid to —" He stopped in mid-sentence, quieted by the look of black rage flashing from Hilton's eyes. "Get on with it," Tanner finished.

Hilton turned his attention back to Roan. "Step out here, McCrae. Like the man said, I've been paid to kill *you*. It's Tanner wants the wolf, not me."

"You're a crazy man, Thax Hilton," Roan replied, watching as his words spawned Hilton's anger. "One day you're a stone cold killer, the next you're not. But I'm coming out as you asked. 'Tis a reasonable request seeing you've accepted the booty for your bloody deed." His fingers tightened on the rifle. He was no fool. Facing Hilton without a gun already in hand would be suicide.

He moved from behind the pine.

To his left, another voice said, "I think it's time we evened the odds here."

Roan watched in awe as a tall, powerfully built Indian moved with ease through the woods. He wore fringed pants and no shirt. His steps were silent despite his size. His moccasins, laced tightly around the brave's muscular calves, were like none Roan had seen before.

He cradled a rifle in his arms and sidled past Roan and into the clearing, the gun barrel pointed directly at Jake Tanner.

From behind Roan and the Indian appeared six more of his people. They moved to stand beside their leader. Each carried a Henry rifle. They stopped a few feet away to face the Double S crew.

Tanner growled, "Falcon, what the hell? You jump the reservation?"

"And if I did? Now that I'm here, I might even start my own war."

Thax Hilton sucked in a deep breath. "I think, Mr. Tanner, that there will come a better day for this business. It's time to depart."

With a sneer, Tanner exploded, "Don't tell me you're afraid of a few dumb Indians."

"I won't then, but neither am I anxious to mix company with them."

"He's a wise man, Tanner," the Indian said. "You would be smart to pay heed to his suggestion." He shifted his attention to Roan. "Would you mind stepping out here?"

Roan hesitated. His only real contact with Indians had been the two times he was with Warren Quade when they visited the Dakota agency. These fellows seemed friendly enough and apparently had no great love for Jake Tanner, but they were the same Dakota Sioux who, a few years back, wiped out an entire regiment of the U.S. Cavalry. Still, if they were of a mind to kill him, they could do it easy enough where he stood.

He walked into the open not quite certain whether to watch Tanner and Hilton or Falcon and his men.

"You're safe enough at the moment," Falcon said. "Any one of these men who lifts a gun will lose blood."

Keeping a distance between them, Roan walked even with him.

"Now," Falcon asked, "do you work for the Double S?"

"Nay."

"Have you ever worked for them?"

"Nay, never."

"Why the hell all the questions, Falcon? Hell no, he never worked for me. Ain't no way I'd have that Irish bastard on our range."

Falcon smiled. "That's good to know, Tanner. I don't usually give a damn about a white man's fight. As far as I'm concerned The People would be better off if you just killed each other."

"Then get out of the way and let us do just that — get rid of the mick" — Tanner cast a look at Hilton's glowering expression and corrected himself — "the Irishman."

"Hear me out," Falcon said. "My people have no love for any white man, but they especially dislike you, Tanner, and your crew of killers." He shouldered the rifle and aimed at Tanner's head. "You have ten seconds to have this bunch headed toward home range."

"Now hold on —" Tanner protested.

"One . . . two —"

"That's all," Hilton said, turning his mount and walking him away. Over his shoulder he said, "Steppe paid me to kill one man. I'm not fighting an Indian war in the bargain. I'm gone."

A chorus of agreement came from the other men. They followed as he rode toward Double S land and left Tanner alone with Roan and the hostile Falcon.

"What are you?" Tanner called after them. "A bunch of damned women?"

"Five . . . six —" Falcon counted.

"Hell with you. Hell with the whole Sioux nation. You don't scare me." Yet, despite his bravado, Tanner gathered the reins and backed his horse a few steps. "You listen to me, *mick*, I ain't through with you yet."

He touched spurs to the sides of his mount and raced off to catch the others.

Chapter Six

Roan sighed in relief and faced Falcon. "Did you feel, friend, Indian, that for just a minute there I was sailing too close to the wind?"

Falcon shook his head. "If that means you were in danger, yes. Tanner is either a cowardly bully or a brave fool. Either way, he's not to be trusted."

"Aye," Roan answered, and studied Falcon's face. Indians, he had always been told, spoke a language all their own, yet here was the second — the first being Tula Moon — who spoke the King's English better than he did. Tula had been educated by the missionaries on the reservation. He supposed this one, this Falcon, had done the same.

"We haven't met before, have we?" Falcon asked. "I don't believe I've ever seen you around these parts."

"Aye, lad, me home —" Fleeting sadness stopped him. He had no home. It lay now nothing more than a heap of ashes. He corrected himself. "What used to be me home was a bit southwest of the Q-C line. Tell me now, is what Tanner said true? You and your lads here truly be from the Sioux reservation?"

Falcon nodded. "We are. But we often hunt on Q-C range when we need fresh meat." He held his finger in the air, a sign that he had more to say. "But only with permission from Warren Quade."

"Ah, you know Mr. Quade then, so you must surely be knowing his housekeeper, and a fair maiden she is — Tula Moon."

Falcon raised an eyebrow. A smile curved his thin lips. "Fair maiden? Not likely anymore."

Roan's face flushed with anger.

A mischievous glint appeared in Falcon's dark eyes. "But she is a lady, that I will admit. Tula Moon is the daughter of my father's brother — my *cousin* as the white man would say."

"Aye," Roan agreed. "A lady. She is that." He held out his hand toward the Indian. "Roan McCrae be the name."

Falcon's grip was strong. "I am called Falcon Claw, most often just Falcon. I was given the name because of these." He raised his hand to indicate three deep scars fanning out from his right eye. "It is said I was born with them."

Strange, Roan thought, the defects didn't really detract from the young man's handsome features, although the eye did appear to be constantly squinting as though from a too-bright sun.

Falcon stared beyond where Roan stood and pointed. "Is he tracking you? Or would you call him friend?"

Patch sat quietly at the edge of the tree line, his bright eyes remaining ever watchful. " 'Tis me friend, Patch. Some wouldn't call him that. They'd rather he be dead. So I'll be taking him to north country, away from the cattle and eager guns."

"Those belonging to the Double S, I assume."

"Aye. And others."

"The Q-C?"

"Aye. Q-C is cattle, same as the other. They'd hesitate not a whit to shoot him on sight, but they don't hunt him down as the likes of Jake Tanner does."

"Maybe you should tell me why Tanner is so anxious to kill the wolf . . . and you."

"He's after killing Patch because of me. He only wants to cause hurt."

"And why do you care so much for a lobo? Is he a pet?"

"Nay, not a pet — a brother."

Falcon frowned. "The People consider every living thing a brother until the creature proves differently, but a white man believing that way? It's unusual."

"Aye, I suppose it is, but, you see, Patch and meself have a kinship in our souls. Like me, he's lost his beloved mate. He understands me grieving days." Roan's voice cracked with emotion. He waited until he could again speak without the hoarseness of sorrow. "There was a time, not too distant, when I wanted him dead as well. Now, knowing he understands me own heart, I'd lay down me life for him. Can you understand that, Mr. Falcon?"

"Only too well. You have the same soul as The People, Roan McCrae, not like Tanner and Azle Steppe. They're well known on the reservation. Land-hungry, greedy and mean to the core. The Sioux despise them."

"Aye," Roan clenched his jaw. "Disliked by meself also."

"Tell me, McCrae, why do men still want you dead when they have taken your property? Otherwise, you would stay and protect it. Surely you wouldn't guard the wolf ahead of the land."

Roan considered the question carefully. "Nay, I would fight for me farm, that's true. And I suppose you could say they've already beaten me there, burned me cabin and run their herd into me fields."

"Then why — ?"

"Tanner's not a man to forget when someone's bested him. I'm not an easy man to beat down. He won't let the times I've sent him packing go without a bit of revenge. He'll not let me be in peace." Roan added, "He knows as well that once Patch is safe, I'll be back to fight for what's me own. Azle Steppe don't want that."

"Fight alone?"

"I'm believing there'll be others to help — the law, Warren Quade."

"And a dozen or more —"

"Not yourself, surely."

Falcon nodded and motioned toward the others. "All of us and a good number more. The Double S men are nothing but trouble. Each time they deliver goods to the reservation, they do as they please. We are allowed no guns on the reservation, but they wear theirs. They shove our young braves around, degrade our women." He laughed bitterly. "We would love to shake the rattles of those snakes."

"But you'd sure find trouble with the agency if you left the reservation?"

"Of course — if they knew we were gone. But who would tell them? You? We often slip away and sometimes we wear the white man's clothing. Who would know?" He smiled, displaying even white teeth. "A Sioux warrior gets bored lying around doing nothing. We crave a good fight." He held his hand out to Roan.

Returning Falcon's smile, Roan accepted the gesture. " 'Tis something to think on and consider, friend Falcon. It's me thanks you've earned."

"And my friendship you've earned, if you'll accept it. Should you ever need help, get word to me by Tula Moon. She visits the reservation often." He gestured for his men to leave. "If we are to catch fresh meat, we must be at it."

With a sure stride, he disappeared into the trees.

Roan retrieved the dun and pack horse to lead them into the clearing. He snapped his fingers and called, "Come, Patch."

His head proudly erect, the wolf bounded forward.

"You know, Patch, me friend, our meeting with those Indians might well be the reckoning of me avenging saint."

In early afternoon, Roan entered what looked like a grassy lea and termed it a good place to let the horses rest and graze. Just as he dismounted, a slight movement a few yards to his right caught his eye. He smiled.

He wouldn't be eating jerked beef the rest of the day. A covey of fool hen grouse, unmindful of his presence, pecked at the earth. They had earned their nickname well. They were indeed foolish fowl, so intent on their stomachs that they failed to guard their lives.

He located a long stick, hefted it a couple of times to get the feel of it in his hand and crept toward the hens. Before they were aware of the intruder in their midst, he clouted two of them. Only then did the others scatter. *Fool hens* indeed they were.

After cleaning the birds, he built a campfire and spit on which he skewered them. Soon the aroma of roasting hens filled his nostrils. His belly rumbled impatiently.

Patch sat a few feet away, watching as Roan turned their dinner over the glowing coals. Occasionally, he would stare at the food then Roan, then back again to the meat. His tongue lashed across his mouth and he whimpered.

Roan laughed. "Me Da used to say patience reaps great reward, me boy. So have a bit of patience."

Patch gave no sign of believing Da's words at that moment. Finally, he settled into a prone position, his eyes never wavering from the cooking birds.

Comfortably fed, Roan followed a game trail

which wound around the lower hog-backed ridge of a high mountain.

Patch maintained the pace a few yards to the right, his bushy tail curled proudly over his back, his head high. He sniffed the air around him as though hoping for another feast of fool hen.

In the distance, echoing from the valley in front of him, the shrill whistle of a bull elk burst forth. From the mountainside opposite came an answering call.

At the lip of the valley, Roan stopped and surveyed the land. Lonely, rugged country with a beauty all its own. He wondered sometimes, as he did now, if even the green of the Erin Isle could equal the panorama before him. The mist embracing the bogs would be little competition to the purple haze hanging over this valley.

Patch's low growl drew his attention away from the beauty. The wolf stiffened. His eyes grew sharp and alert. His ruff and mane stood straight up. He snarled, revealing long fangs.

"What is it, me friend? What's got your hackles up?"

The dun shied, nearly throwing Roan from his back. "What in the shades of the devil hisself is happening here?"

From around a boulder not twenty feet away, his answer came — a grizzly, one of the biggest he had ever seen. Roan slowly reached for the rifle.

The bear roared and lumbered toward him.

Just as Roan's hand felt the firm wood of the butt, the dun reared and twisted to the side, throwing Roan from the saddle and into the path of the charging bear.

Although stunned, he gained his footing and staggered to the side. The grizzly lifted one powerful paw and struck. The paw landed on Roan's left shoulder and clung. He felt himself drawn closer to the giant.

Somewhere in the back of his mind, he heard Katie's voice, as he had so many times, saying her beads, "Holy Mary, mother of God —" It had been so long since he felt close to God, to the church.

A second blow rained down on him, striking him in the chest, hurling him backward. Another followed, which slammed into his rib cage. Roan collapsed on the ground. "Pray for us sinners —" he whispered, gasping for air.

The bear charged. Roan screamed. Wet fur smothered him. Stinking hot breath made him gag. Long teeth sank into his already wounded shoulder. The beast lifted him from the ground. Pain shot through his arm as if it had been ripped from his body.

". . . now and at the hour of our death. Amen. Hail Mary —"

As suddenly as the attack began, it ended. The grizzly loosened its grip and threw him aside as it might have an empty honeycomb.

Roan needed the rifle. With difficulty he lifted his head and peered through tear-clouded eyes to search for the dun. When we saw it, his heart sank. Along with the pack horse, the dun raced frantically down the back trail.

". . . full of grace. Blessed art thou —"

The grizzly roared, but the sound was a distance away. Pain in Roan's side took his breath, but somehow he managed to roll toward the noise. When his eyes focused on the sight, he moaned and called, "Patch, come!" His words died in his throat.

Patch arced through the air and jumped astraddle the bear's broad back. His front paws gripped the grizzly's shoulder hump. His teeth sank into one of the animal's ears. Blood spurted over the bear's matted fur and Patch's muzzle.

Roan put his hands over his ears, trying to close out the snarling from Patch's throat, the roar of the angered grizzly. Certain Patch would die, Roan closed his eyes and prayed more fervently. "Blessed is the fruit of thy womb —"

The bear jerked its head and ripped its injured ear from Patch's hold. Patch growled and snapped down on the other ear, ripping it loose from the massive head. The bear roared in agony, tried to shake his attacker loose.

Patch sank his fangs into the thick neck.

The grizzly reared on its hind legs with Patch clinging to its back.

The bear twisted, ripping its hide as Patch landed on the ground with a chunk of the bear's skin still in his mouth. The wolf spit out the distasteful bite and retreated a few feet. Pulling lips back from bloody canines, he snarled a threat.

The grizzly launched another charge. Patch leaped out of the way and circled until he was behind his adversary. He attacked the bear's hindquarters. The great beast twisted and swatted at Patch, who again hit hard, retreated and hit again. In only seconds, the grizzly's rump, ripped and matted, bled profusely. He bellowed and rolled his huge head.

He had had enough. With one final roar, he dashed for the valley below. Patch raced behind him, still nipping at the offending rear.

Racking pain tore through Roan. For the first time, he examined his wounds. His shirt was ripped into long strips stained red with his own blood. Three deep gashes slashed their way across his chest. Blood trickled from his torn shoulder. Two more gashes exposed his ribs.

Dizziness overtook him. The blood oozed too fast. If he couldn't stop it somehow, he would die. With agonizing effort, he pulled handfuls of grass, packing them against the wounds and used strips of his shirt to secure them. He shoved his hand inside his belt, holding his arm tightly against the bleeding wounds in his side.

Movement weakened him. Beads of sweat collected on his face and rolled down into the gaping chest wounds, the sting from the salt causing even more pain. His right arm felt heavy, too heavy to lift.

He struggled to his feet, his legs trembling. He

knew damned well he hadn't stopped his life ebbing away, only prolonged it a little. He had to get help, but . . . where? The reservation? Q-C?

He couldn't remember how far he had traveled or exactly where he was. His only chance was the dun, but the grizzly had frightened the horse so much, he was probably still running. Roan had to take the slim chance. He headed down the valley trail, his steps uncertain, his vision clouded. Inside his head, a drum throbbed and he realized it was his heart pumping the life from him.

"Holy Mary —" he whispered.

Chapter Seven

Something, someone still stalked Roan. He stumbled and almost fell as he searched for whatever was behind him on the trail. At the sight of Patch, he drew a relieved breath. So enveloped was he in his own predicament, in the intensity of the pain, he had forgotten his friend.

He looked the wolf over. One forepaw was mangled. Patch whimpered at Roan's light touch. "The beasty got you good, didn't he, me friend? Well, we'll get you fixed up and soon."

Patch snorted.

"You're really a wonder, me friend. It's me life I'm owing to you, boy, and a thanks for it. I only hope I can favor you with your own life, saints be willing and I live."

He snapped his fingers and headed once again down the trail, Patch following only a few feet behind. "We got to find them horses," Roan said.

Patch whimpered in reply.

Roan stumbled along the path, keeping himself upright with a heavy stick. He followed the trail by the dim light of a gibbous moon.

What seemed like hours later, he entered the lea where he'd been earlier in the day — or had it been yesterday? He wasn't sure. Never had he been so weary or thirsty. And to add to his woes, chill from fever had overtaken him halfway down the trail.

He tried to recall whether he had left wood

near his campfire site. A fire would help, of that he was certain. His muddled mind urged him to find kindling and warm himself by the flame. His common sense urged him on.

His thirst was unbearable, brought on by the loss of blood and the fevered sweat. He had to have water and there was none in the lea that he recalled. But he did remember crossing a stream yesterday . . . or the day before . . . or months ago.

He pushed himself onward one step at a time, one breath at a time.

The soft nicker of a horse stopped him in his tracks.

The pack horse shuffled out of the trees a few yards away. Roan stifled a cry of joy until he saw the limping gait as the animal favored its right hind leg.

For a moment, the misty shroud in his mind lifted. He stumbled to the horse's side and slid his hand over the leg. He found no crippling injury. A sigh of relief escaped. The horse's pack had slipped — probably caught on a tree branch, loosening the rope — and was now shoved so far back on the hindquarter, it had all but immobilized the leg.

He grabbed the lead rope, muttered a thanks to his saints and groped through the pack for the canteen. He prayed it hadn't been lost or punctured.

Frantic moments passed. He ignored the reason his arm was held tightly against him. He freed his hand and searched again for the casque of water. The sound of someone sobbing broke through his panic. He turned his head only to find it was the sound of his own fear.

Taking deep breaths to calm himself, he searched beneath the horse's belly and found the canteen nearly dragging the ground. He slashed the rope, uncorked the casque and lifted it to his lips. He downed three long swallows before his stomach protested. He gagged and struggled to keep the fluid down.

"I be a damn fool!" he cursed himself. "Knowing the better and I swig like a *pub hog* without his whiskey. It's slow I must drink. There's no need to waste the supply."

His innards protested with mild nausea. His thoughts turned to untying the pack bindings, allowing the horse to graze, but his hands were too weak, too shaky. Irritated at his own weakness, he slashed the ropes and let the pack fall.

He dug out the battered tin pan and poured water for Patch. When the wolf had his fill, Roan did the same for the horse.

He could do no more. He pulled the tarp from the pack and wrapped himself in it. Needles of ice, borne along on the night wind, pricked his body.

The smell of his own blood made his stomach roil. A coughing spasm seized him and tore open the wounds he had sealed with grass. Racking pain overcame him. He slipped into unconsciousness.

Roan wasn't sure what awakened him. Maybe the bright sunlight warming his face, causing him to sweat inside the heavy tarp, aggravating the wounds.

Maybe . . . he strained to listen . . . maybe the horses approaching, their hooves vibrating the ground beneath him.

He raised his head enough to see riders coming down the ground rise back of the trees. They slowed as they approached the wooded area surrounding the lea.

The night's rest had cleared Roan's mind a little, but the pain intensified and the fog it brought hovered on the edge of his consciousness.

Ignoring the searing discomfort, he pulled himself to a sitting position and searched the area for Patch. As always, he sat on his haunches only a few feet away. His attention, like Roan's, was on the approaching riders.

He growled, his lips drawn back, baring his fangs.

"Patch!" Roan commanded. "Run!"

The wolf regarded him with an expression that assured Roan he understood, but he remained where he was.

"Go, Patch! Now!" Roan snapped his fingers and pointed. "Faith, old son, I know you want to help, but you can't do it if you're dead. Get yourself out of here! Begone with you!"

Patch obeyed, disappearing into the trees just

as the first rider emerged. "I might have known it'd be the likes of you, Jake Tanner," Roan said. Behind him, Azle Steppe and Thax Hilton now appeared. Another man led Roan's dun. He suspected there would be another hand or two, probably hidden in the woods. Steppe seldom traveled without plenty of guns.

Tanner leaned his arms across the saddle pommel and smirked. "Well, well, well. Would you look what we got here? Where's your wolf friend, McCrae?"

Roan ignored the question. He leaned on his right arm, letting his gaze travel over Steppe and Hilton, finally resting on the rider holding the dun's reins.

"I see you found me horse."

Tanner dismounted and moved to stand menacingly over Roan. "We backtracked him here," he snarled. "I asked you where that damned wolf was."

Still ignoring him, Roan struggled to his feet, his jaw clenched so tight with the effort it ached. He would not, he told himself stubbornly, allow Tanner — or any of them for that matter — to know the pain he suffered.

A wave of dizziness thwarted his efforts. He staggered backward to keep from falling.

Steppe leaned forward in his saddle. "You going to answer the question?"

Roan sneered, but said nothing.

"You'll either answer or I'll have Hilton here gut shoot you."

Roan glared beneath brows drawn into a frown. He would be damned if he'd show fear. He took a step toward Tanner. "Move," he ordered. "I want me horse."

Tanner stood his ground, a sinister smile on his face. "Move me," he replied.

"For the love of God, Tanner," Hilton cut in. "The man's hurt badly from the looks of him."

"Damned if he ain't." Tanner broke into an evil laugh. "Guess it's my turn now."

He swung his fist toward Roan, who saw the movement and ducked, but the loss of blood, the constant pain slowed his reaction. The sledge-hammer blow landed high on his temple and spun him halfway around.

Jolting daggers of agony stabbed his body as he fell on his wounded left side. He moaned and fought the darkness that slowly engulfed him.

Tanner laughed again. Someone grabbed Roan's hair and lifted his head.

A voice — Hilton's voice — echoed through the tunnel of fog that now surrounded him. "Tanner, you rotten bastard —"

The darkness won. Roan drifted into it and remained.

Consciousness returned slowly. Voices, hollow and far away, vibrated in Roan's ears. He opened his eyes, but only blurred forms swam before him. Drums pounded inside his head. He lay still waiting for his vision to clear, for the voices to take on substance.

Thax Hilton's deep tones bored through the buzzing in Roan's ears. "Here's your blood money, Azle Steppe. Every rotten penny of it."

Roan struggled to raise his head. The figures were still indistinct, but he thought he saw Tanner, his big frame motionless on the ground. Hilton stood in front and to the side of Azle Steppe's mount.

"You will regret this action, Hilton," Steppe said gruffly. He shifted in his saddle and leaned forward. "I intend owning a hundred square miles of rangeland real soon. It's going to take tough men to get it, men who know how to use their guns. You could be number one there, Hilton. Regrettable."

"I don't gun down sick men or animals that have done me no harm. Now, Mr. Steppe, if you don't want to lose Tanner, too, may I suggest you load him on his horse and get him to a doctor? I gave him more than a slight tap on his head."

Steppe motioned to two men behind him. They lifted Tanner from the ground and carried him to his horse. One of the men, his tone uncertain, said, "I don't know, boss. He looks dead to me. Head's sure bloody."

"Nonsense," Steppe answered. "You can't kill a man like Jake Tanner with a pistol whipping."

He picked up the reins to Tanner's horse and urged his own mount a few steps forward until he towered over Roan. "Irishman, you listen good. I'll have you dead yet." He turned toward

Hilton. "And you, mister, you'll die, too. No one leaves my employ unless I tell them to — especially your kind."

One of the men who had loaded Tanner on his horse shouted, "Why don't you let me do it now, boss? I never did like niggers much."

Steppe whirled toward him. "You shut your damn mouth. There's not a man jack among you could do the job alone. Hilton would have half of you dead before one of you got a slug in him. Let's go!" He put spurs to his mount and led his crew toward the mountains.

Roan and Hilton remained silent until the riders were out of sight. Only then did Hilton kneel beside Roan to assess the shredded, blood-soaked shirt. "Mister, you look like you escaped from hell and the devil's still looking for you. Can you sit a horse or shall I build a travois?"

"You get me in that saddle. I'll do me best to stay there."

Hilton lifted a shred of Roan's shirt and peered beneath it. "I suppose there's a good reason for the grass."

"Packing. Had to stop the bleeding."

"Hmmm. The wolf do this?"

Roan shook his head, then wished he hadn't. The movement sent rivers of agony coursing through him. "Grizzly," he said, the pain taking his breath. "Hadn't been for Patch, this lad would be meeting the bog angels for certain."

"Patch?"

"Me wolf friend. Chewed that bear up and spit

him back out again."

Hilton nodded, a disbelieving grin on his face. "You're telling me a wolf attacked a grizzly and the wolf won?"

"It's that I'm telling you right enough."

"Never heard of such a thing."

"And I'd never seen such, but it was a real sight, one I won't be forgetting in me lifetime."

"And where's this bear-killer now?"

"I sent him away when I seen the likes of you coming. He's not gone far." Roan turned to scan the tree line. Patch sat just at the edge of the clearing, watching, waiting.

Roan whistled. "Come, Patch. Come here to me."

The wolf trotted toward them, his eyes regarding Hilton. He stopped a few feet away and no amount of coaxing would draw him nearer. He growled.

Hilton's hands eased to the butts of his revolvers.

Patch's growl became a threatening snarl.

"You'd best be dropping your hands, Mr. Hilton. He's not certain of your loyalties just yet."

Hilton dropped his hands to his sides and stood, motionless, his black eyes mirroring Patch's apprehension.

"It's been a good while since I fed me friends," Roan told him. "So, before you put the pack on me horse, would you be so kind as to give me dun some grain?"

91

Still eyeing the wolf, Hilton backed toward the grain sack, dumped a sizable amount for the horses and stayed where he was.

"You want something to eat, too, McCrae?" he asked.

"Aye. A portion of that dried beef would do me fine. And, if you don't mind, would you give me friend Patch one of them steaks? Perhaps he'd take kindlier to you after that."

Thax handed Roan the jerked beef, unwrapped a steak and held it toward the wolf.

Patch growled, baring his fangs.

"I won't dispute your word, McCrae, but I'm not seeing any close friendship developing here."

Roan snapped his fingers. "Come, Patch. Eat."

The wolf edged closer, an inch or two at a time.

Hilton held the steak at arm's length.

"It's me feeling that the both of you are stubborn as a moor rat. You got no intention of moving that steak closer to his mouth and he don't seem inclined to bring his mouth to meet the steak."

"So what do you suggest?"

"That one or the other of you stop playing the jackass."

Hilton laughed. His tensed muscles eased noticeably and he moved forward toward Patch, who waited. When Hilton came near, only then did Patch rise to accept the offered food. He clamped his teeth into the steak, turned and limped to the edge of the woods before tearing into it.

"He's your friend now for sure, Mr. Hilton."

"I certainly hope so. I would hate to have that big beast as an enemy."

"Perhaps you'd be so good as to fix up that wounded paw of his now that you be brothers."

"Get something straight, McCrae. I have few friends and I am damn sure no brother to a wolf. He'll heal himself — a lot better than you will, I'm sure."

" 'Tis a shame then, Thaxter Hilton. Me friend Patch is a good companion to ride the trails with. To be brother to such would be an honorable thing."

"Cousin maybe," Hilton said. A smile creased his dark face.

Roan chewed, with effort, on the dried beef. His thirst mounted again. What he wouldn't give for a cup of hot coffee or the herb tea Katie used to brew for him on cool autumn evenings. He gave voice to his longing.

"Why didn't you say before that you wanted tea?" Hilton asked.

"You're saying it would have done me some good with the scant belongings I brought with me?"

Hilton grinned, lifted himself from his resting place on a flat-topped rock and ambled into the woods. Within minutes he returned, his big hand wrapped around a bouquet of yellow flowers.

"Saints be!" Roan said. "I ask for tea and the man brings me posies."

Without a word, Hilton stripped the leaves

from the plants into the tin pan and poured water from the canteen. He built a small fire and set the pot to steep. From his own horse, he lifted a canvas sack and withdrew two drinking cups, filling one for Roan, the other for himself.

Roan sipped the hot brew and let it flow through him and the intensity of the pain eased for the first time since the grizzly attacked. "You're a good man to have around, Mr. Hilton. It's thankful I am that you saw fit to give Azle Steppe his money back."

Hilton remained silent, but his expression was one of a man deep in thought.

"Tell me, why did you quit the likes of Steppe? You were paid to kill me and it'd have been easy enough."

The reply came slowly, thoughtfully. "I'm not sure I can tell you why. From the first day I took the job, I was uncomfortable."

"But you don't know why?"

"Maybe it was you. You got more sand in that craw of yours than anyone I ever met."

"You got a whit of sand yourself, Mr. Hilton, and that's a fact. But you trouble me some."

"How so?"

"I've been away from me own land only a few years and, in Ireland, no man had skin like yours — like the dust from the coal mines, it is."

Hilton stiffened at the mention of his color.

"I'm wondering why your black skin seems to anger people like Steppe and Tanner so much."

With a shrug, Hilton answered, "They're ignorant. Ignorant people dislike anyone who is different. I'm different."

"It's a fact, you are. So am I, I guess, in a way that gives you and meself a sort of kinship."

"Kinship?" Hilton said doubtfully.

"Like me brother Patch there. He's me kind, too. So, if you've a mind to stick with me, Mr. Hilton, I'll have me wolf brother and me black brother." He held out his hand.

Hesitating only a moment, Hilton accepted the gesture, a grin lighting his face. "I knew the first time I met you, Roan McCrae, that you were a man with a gift for intelligence — horse sense, I've always called it. You seem bound to make me a part of that wolf's family. Well, it would be my pleasure to accept this brotherhood you offer."

"Done then. Now would you kindly be helping me into the saddle. I think me blood is leaking out faster than me body can replace it. I'm feeling none too well."

Hilton's smile faded into concern. He lifted Roan to his feet and struggled him into the saddle. As they headed for help, Roan had time only to glance at Patch, who remained at the edge of the woods, watching them ride away.

He heard Hilton snap his fingers and call, "Come, Patch."

He knew, somehow, the wolf responded, but Roan never saw him fall in step with the horses.

Chapter Eight

Dark and light, light and dark. Roan roamed in and out of the two, believing somehow the darkness was night, the light was day. Thax Hilton led the way, holding the reins to Roan's mount. During the light time, Roan tried to make conversation, but his tongue felt swollen and useless.

Once he managed to croak out, "Stream . . . saw a stream . . . cool water . . . lay down in it."

Hilton answered, but his words got lost in the darkness.

Patch was always there in the light, walking close beside Roan's dun, then the dark would fall and Patch would wander away.

Pain was ever present, too, unrelenting, each jolt of the horse's gait jarring sharp spikes through Roan's side.

Hilton's face appeared again. "Hold on," it said, but there was nothing to hold on to and he fell into the dark.

Once, during the period of light, he heard water trickling. He tried to tell Hilton the stream was ahead, but his voice failed and he was afraid they would ride on by with Hilton never noticing the cool water.

The rippling sound drew closer. Fine spray misted Roan's face . . . or was it only cold sweat? The dun halted suddenly and strong arms lifted Roan from the saddle. He focused for a scant second of wide, dark eyes with whites like the new-fallen snow in the Montana mountains and black skin glistening.

With a suddenness that startled him fully awake, he had the sensation of floating in a bed of cool water. It flowed across his burning chest and side and soothed the pain. Clear water . . . burbling away from him . . . turned red and ugly as it wandered on its course.

Another face appeared above him — not Hilton's. This one was dark, too, but more the color of the iron-fed soil, coppery and smooth. A voice said something about a Falcon. A rush of fear shot through Roan at the thought of being carried away in the talons of a great bird.

Then the talons sank into his side and lifted him from the cooling water. He knew it was too late.

The dark time had come.

Darkness subsided into blinding white light at the end of a tunnel, like a hole in the pain.

He could ease his body through that hole. But each time he reached for the opening, the light moved beyond his grasp.

Cold enveloped his body, cold so intense that it formed icicles across the hole of light and he couldn't squeeze himself between them.

Shrouded suddenly by mist, sometimes nothing more than a gossamer veil, other times so thick it hid the hole of light, he drifted. The thickness wrapped around him, laid him in a bed of orange-hot embers. His tongue swelled and filled his mouth and throat so he couldn't breathe.

The icicles melted and metamorphosed into iron bars, glowing red and yellow like the embers amid the white light, now more blinding than ever. The light and the bars spiraled toward him. They circled above him until they became a face, hideous, terrifying.

A long hooked beak formed the nose and mouth. Curled horns were the ears and wings, covered with glistening black feathers beat up and down, hovering just above his face. They buzzed like a rattler's warning.

Moans, like a melody from hell, escaped from the beak, punctuated by ear-splitting shrieks.

He wanted to break loose, to escape from the face, the beak, but he remained paralyzed. The creature hovered over him so close he could smell its stinking breath. Even when it rose again, out of his reach, the fetid odor remained.

As suddenly as it had appeared, the face faded. The wings no longer fanned him with their heat. The rattler crawled away, the sound of its anger diminished.

Another face appeared, this one as beautiful as the first was terrifying. Dark eyes glistened with raindrops. Gentle words dripped from the wide mouth. Soft lips touched his face with healing coolness.

The smell lingered for only a moment after the angel came to protect him then wafted into a pleasant scent of cool spring water.

As if by the magic of the little people, his body rose, light and unfettered by pain. Floating upward, he passed through the hole and between the bars which now had turned to sticks tied together so they stuck out at angles all around the hole.

On the other side, night, sprinkled with bright stars and a waning moon, closed around him.

He looked below, where he lay before and saw the ring of burning embers. Then the angel's wings touched his face, surrounding him in a soft drape of comfort.

And he slept.

Roan awakened to the sound of a child whimpering nearby. Still lost in thick fog, he felt around him for the baby. He wanted to touch, to comfort, to soothe the intensity of its sorrow.

His fingers touched the soft fur — a blanket, he was certain — and he searched for the child, finding only a beast's head, the throat vibrating with the whimpering.

The fog lifted a little. Above him he could see a tipi's smoke hole. The light sifting through the opening seemed less intense than before, the sticks less ominous. Walls made of hides enclosed him. Hot embers burned nearby.

A brief memory of Falcon floated into his mind and he realized where he was. Of course, Hilton would have brought him to the reservation, would have taken the nearest help available.

Whimpering, louder now, interrupted his thoughts and he stroked the wolf's fur. Patch moved. His big head nuzzled against Roan's burning side. A warm tongue lapped at Roan's hand. The stroking brought with it reality. Roan turned his head, forced a smile and tried to speak. His voice barely audible, he whispered, "Patch, me friend, 'tis good knowing you're all right."

Patch crowded closer. His body stretched along Roan's as though he was afraid if the touching stopped so would the friendship.

"The devil be riding too close this time, Patch, but, by the saints when they be willing, we'll try again. I'll not let a bullet put you down. You keep yourself close until I be well again. You understand?"

From Patch's throat came a half-groan, half-whimper in reply.

The tipi flap parted. Falcon stepped inside, tying the opening back to let in the morning light. Hilton followed. Both moved to Roan's side and seated themselves cross-legged on the floor.

"Would you look at this, Falcon?" Hilton said. "The old son of the sod finally woke up."

Falcon laughed, but his laughter held more concern than humor. *"Hec-ta,* finally. When we left you last night, my friend Roan McCrae, you were sleeping like a suckling papoose. How do you feel, *Tac-se-nas?"*

"Is it meself or Patch you be talking to?" Roan asked.

"It is you. I know how that wolf is. He tore the hole you see in the side of my tipi after the first day. You were only half-conscious. I thought he intended to attack Oien-ta when he first commenced his medicine on you."

"Oien-Ta?"

"Our shaman — doctor you might call him, our medicine man. He gave you your new name — *Tac-se-nas*."

Roan made a feeble effort to raise himself to a sitting position. Pain forced him back. Sweat dotted his brow and a soft moan escaped his lips.

"I wouldn't be trying that again too soon," Hilton said. "You're far from well."

"Faith, I believe you. But me curiosity is up. Until now Roan McCrae has been me only name, a fine name, me Da give it to me when I was born. Why, in the love of heaven, did your — what did you call him? — shaman? — give me a new one? And one I can't pronounce at that."

Falcon smiled and nudged Hilton. "You tell him."

Hilton's white teeth gleamed as he grinned. "Well, from what Tula Moon tells me —"

"Tula? She's here?"

Hilton's expression turned serious. "You don't remember? You're a strange man, McCrae. Pretty woman like that cried over me like she has you, I'd remember. You can believe that."

"Aye," Roan answered. "The angel with raindrops in her eyes."

"He's still out of it, Falcon. Angel with raindrops. That make sense to you?"

"Enough!" Roan interrupted. "A dream, it was. I seen the likes of Tula Moon in me dream."

"Some dream," Hilton said. "Anyway, she says

you are usually a man who speaks little unless you have something important to say. But no one would have believed the first three days after we brought you here."

"Three days?"

"And more. Look, my man, would you let me finish this story. My God, you're still chattering. I don't think Tula knows you as well as she thinks she does."

"Then continue your story and it's a little quieter I'll be."

"The old shaman named you Tac-se-nas because you talked all the time. Right, Falcon?"

"Right." Falcon leaned closer, whispering as he might to a conspirator. "It means one-who-talks-too-much. Oien-Ta said the spirit of *Qua-Qua-Shee*, the quarreling magpie, had entered you along with a few other bad spirits I'd almost forgotten existed. He nearly wore the wings off his ceremonial cape trying to drive them out."

"Aye. That was in me dream also." Roan sighed. His eyelids grew heavy. He fought to keep them open.

"I think we'd best leave now," Hilton told him, "and let you get some rest."

Falcon followed him through the tipi opening, saying as he left, "It's good to see you growing stronger, friend Roan. You had us worried."

"Aye. I worried a bit meself." He fell asleep before he could ask the many questions that crowded his mind.

The touch of cool fingers on his forehead brought him around again, shrouded this time in the thick mist. Katie lay next to him, her head cradled on her arm, her eyes watching him.

She smiled and leaned toward him. Her lips brushed his softly. That she had come back to him seemed no mystery at the moment, but his heart skipped when she raised her head so he could look full in her face.

It wasn't Katie at all. It was Tula Moon. "Why, lass?" he whispered.

"Sh-h-h," she said. "I've wanted to do that, to kiss you, since they told me you awoke this morning."

The voice, husky and melodic, was Tula's, but the face again belonged to Katie, framed by soft auburn tresses and set off by eyes so green they looked as though they were fashioned from the green grass of the old sod.

"What time is it?" he asked.

"Evening. It's been a long day." She kissed him again — Tula did. Confused and uncertain of his feelings, he said nothing more.

"I must tell you something," Tula said. "Please, just listen. I know you understand little of my people. Our culture, our ancestry, our language, but we are not secretive people. You must understand the depth of our devotion to friends, to those we love. We mate for a lifetime."

"Why are you telling me this?"

She brushed the backs of her fingers along his

stubbled cheek. "I want you to understand me, Roan McCrae. *Onca-ate-wakan-loda.*"

Roan blinked against the mist that floated into his mind again. " 'Tis a wonder and mystery you are, lass. Where did you learn such words?"

Katie smiled. "It means you are the spirit of my life. It means I love you."

"Nay, lass, you can't mean that. You left me . . . so lonely . . . so —"

Katie's auburn hair changed suddenly to long black braids plaited with bright beads. Her blue eyes darkened to brown and her fair face faded, drawing further and further from him. He thought, for a minute, the wind sighed through her lips, saying a final goodbye.

"Katie?" he called, but only Tula's voice answered.

"It's all right, Roan. Rest. I shouldn't have spoken of love, not now, but —"

"Then it was you, not me Katie."

"Does that disappoint you?"

"Nay. Only, surely you can't mean what you said. Yourself and me friend, Warren Quade have —"

"Have never said we loved each other," she finished.

"But there's a devotion there. You've been like a mate."

"He missed his wife, grieved for her for two years, then he realized I was a woman. Yes, there's devotion."

"Are you saying you don't love him?"

"I thought for a while I did. It took that time to know I only felt sorry for him. As for Warren, he could never love anyone but Josie and his ranch. That ranch is his life."

"Does he know?"

"That I love you? I don't know. He asked me after you were there the last time. I guess I was too quiet."

"And you told him right out, that it was me you loved?"

"No. I wasn't really sure — not until Falcon came and told me you were hurt, maybe dying."

His eyes felt heavy. Some of what the woman beside him had said, whether it be a dream or not, whirled around inside his brain, taunting him with its invitation. Still, the words were spoken in the fog, a little clearer maybe than before, but nevertheless in the fog.

As though thinking of it brought about a thickening of the haze, it moved in on Roan again, obscuring his surroundings.

Katie's face swam in the distant sea of vision. He wanted to reach for her, to fold his arms around her, but his hands were like lead weights.

"I'm sorry" was all he could think to say.

"Sleep," she said.

And he did.

" 'Twas a lovely dream I had," Roan said when he awakened much later, to a cool morning breeze and the sun warming the inside of the tipi.

The mist had lifted and much of the pain had abated.

Patch lay beside him, sleeping, moving only when Roan moved and then just enough to find comfort again and return to his sleep. Abruptly, the wolf stiffened and, without a second's hesitation, slithered out through the tear in the tipi.

Tula Moon stepped through the entry flap and fussed with the bandage on Roan's chest, smoothing the white cloth in place. Her eyes misted with tears. "Yes, a lovely dream," she answered, almost inaudibly.

"I didn't know you heard me," Roan admitted, his voice weak, hoarse.

She said no more, only turned to tend a pot boiling over the fire.

Carefully, she ladled out the hot broth into a bowl, returned and held it to Roan's lips. "This broth has kept you alive these past days, but it is time you ate more — perhaps some meat."

He managed a weak grin. "Is that venison stew I'm smelling in the big pot over there?"

"It is. For later." She turned away again.

"You're crying, Tula girl. Is it for me you're shedding them tears?"

She shook her head. "White men say Indians don't cry."

"I'd heard that, but it's surely not true. I'm seeing the tears in your dear eyes this very minute. What's making you sad?"

Her back stiffened. "I've spoken the words of my heart to you, Roan McCrae. I spoke them because I thought you were on your journey into death and I needed to give them to you to take with you. It is the way of The People."

"Now you're sorry you said them, is that it?"

"No, Roan, not sorry. Perhaps I opened the mouth of the grave so you could bury a ghost."

"You mean me Katie?"

"In your fever, it was her name you called."

"Even so, Tula girl, you must know I've always —"

"There's only emptiness inside you, Roan. No one could ever fill it. Not now anyway."

He relaxed against the flood of dizziness that swept over him. When the spell passed, he grasped her wrist and pulled her down beside him. "Now, lass, you listen to me. Since I been here in this place I been drifting in and out of me mind. It's only fitting that words of love would bring back me Katie."

She drew in a deep breath, exhaled it in what could only be described as an eternal sigh. "I opened my heart in the face of death, Roan. And now the Lifegiver has erased the death. We will never again speak of what passed between us."

"But —"

She placed her fingertips against his lips to silence him. "It is the way of my people that one does not desert obligations for selfish reasons. Warren Quade has been good to me — kind, generous. I have pledged to him, in his need, my loyalty. I will honor that pledge."

"Then you're telling me, girl, that I'm to be

107

alone again — without me Katie, without you?"

She nodded. "If you want to remain my friend — and Warren's, you will forget the words I spoke."

"You're saying 'never,' is that it?"

"Not as long as Warren lives. And to wish for his death would be my ruin . . . and yours."

Roan pressed against the blankets beneath him. He stared at the tipi opening above, the prison bars in his dream, feeling as though she had condemned him to remain forever in that prison.

The conversation nearly forgotten, Tula turned back to the pot of stew.

"I'll do me best, Tula girl," Roan said. "I'll be keeping your vow to me friend Quade. But 'tis a miserable life you're offering me."

She smiled at him over her shoulder. "Friends have a way of dissolving misery, Roan. I'll always be your friend."

He tried to return the smile, but the effort was lost in her final words.

"— And so will Warren."

Chapter Nine

Tula looked up from cleaning Roan's wounds as Hilton and Falcon entered the tipi. Wordlessly, they seated themselves and watched.

Roan gritted his teeth against the pain as Tula bathed the lacerations with steaming hot water.

"Still looks pretty bad," Falcon commented finally. "But I wonder what shape Roan would be in if old Oien-Ta hadn't applied his horse manure method so quickly."

"Horse manure!" Roan thundered.

Tula patted his cheek. "It's all right, Roan. That old witch doctor is aging and too set in his ways to accept newer methods — especially if the old ones work — gruesome as it may sound."

"But horse manure. My God, girl, horse manure, was it?"

She turned to her cousin. Her eyes narrowed accusingly. "You had to open your mouth, didn't you? You tell him, Falcon. It makes me ill to think about it."

Hilton laughed. "Go ahead, Falcon, I'd like to hear this. Horse manure?"

Falcon, at first, kept his expression serious in the stoic Indian tradition, but a smile tugged at his lips. "All right, you go ahead and laugh — all of you, but time and again, Oien-Ta's remedies did their job. You know once we got Roan here, his wounds were infected and the infection was already spreading. Oien-Ta looked at the cuts and knew. He started applying fresh hot manure. The heat and minerals in the" — he searched for a word and grinned impishly as he thought of one — "shit drew the infection back to the opening of the wound and held it there. He kept the treatment up for two or three days. Then Tula got here."

"Tula, lass." Roan grasped her hand. "Your coming surely saved me life, then, is that not the fact?"

Falcon shook his head. "It's just that she brought some new medication, a salve, but Oien-Ta didn't have any such thing. No Indian did, so we've always trusted in the *Wakanda* of nature. After two or three days, with the horse dung in place, the maggots did the rest."

"Maggots!" Roan shrieked, lifting himself from the pallet. "Sweet Mary, Mother of Jesus," he moaned.

Tula pushed him back down.

"Amen to that," Hilton said. "Maggots in a living body. Great God Almighty."

Falcon nodded his head vigorously. "It's a fact, isn't it, Tula?"

"Yes," she snapped. "Would you hurry and finish your telling? I'm getting ill just listening to you."

"It's simple." Falcon grinned. "Infection is dead flesh, isn't it? And dead flesh is what maggots thrive on. After a few days the wound is scraped and washed clean. What you have left is raw, new flesh — flesh that will heal." He leaned closer to Tula, teasing her. "You also have a great hole in your body that never fills in. But you are alive."

Hilton's eyes widened, then narrowed again, fixing Falcon with a steady gaze. "Sounds unbelievable, my friend. Do you actually know anyone who has been cured by such an unpalatable method?"

"Of course I do," Falcon answered. "Oien-Ta himself. Years ago he was in a skirmish with the Crows. Caught an arrow right in his ass." He threw his head back and laughed heartily. His laughter was contagious. "Can't you just see that old man jumping up and down holding the cheeks of his butt with that arrow sticking straight out, quivering?" He made a quick up and down gesture with his hand.

Roan groaned with the pain of laughter. He gripped his wounded side.

Thax Hilton rolled over backward, his hands pressed tightly against his stomach.

Tula, who tried to pretend she found nothing funny, couldn't hide the undulating of her shoulders as she stifled the giggles. She quickly wiped her eyes. "You stop that this instant, Falcon. Roan isn't well enough for your antics."

An expression of feigned innocence on his face, Falcon controlled his raucous guffaws. "Sorry, Roan."

" 'Tis sorry you need not be, me fine friend. Me Da always said merriment was a better medicine than man could make."

Falcon slapped Hilton on the leg. "Let's go to Oien-Ta's lodge."

"Why?"

"He's got stories to tell that will twist your ears off."

"I'm sure he does," Hilton said, still chuckling. "But I don't speak or understand his language."

"He can speak some English — well enough you can understand him. When he wants you to, that is."

Hilton shrugged, grinning. "Lead the way." He glanced toward Roan. "This may be an interesting visit. I haven't laughed like this in —" His face grew suddenly serious, his eyes taking on a faraway look as he finished lamely, "too long."

"Falcon's good medicine," Roan said.

"He is that," Hilton agreed.

"We'll see you two later." Falcon waved, stepping through the tipi opening, followed closely by Hilton. As they walked away, Falcon's deep voice, filled with good humor, promised, "I tell you, Hilton, old Oien-Ta has a hole in the cheek of his butt you could lay your hand in."

Hilton's low laughter finally dissipated as the two moved beyond Roan's hearing range.

He turned to Tula. "It's a fun-loving young man, that Falcon is."

"He's always been that way. When he was only a gangling youngster, his devilment had the tribal chief and the council at a loss constantly." Sadness clouded her eyes. "But he was born too late."

"Could you be explaining that to the likes of me?"

"The reservation has robbed him of his freedom. It's far too tame."

"But he seems to come and go as he wants."

"True, but he spends a lot of time in the reservation stockade. Rules here don't allow the young braves to wander outside the boundaries. When Falcon is caught —"

"Still, he laughs and joshes. Sure and he can't be so unhappy as you say."

Tula smiled wanly. "A falcon is hard to tame — but it can be done."

A barely audible sound stirred the flap of the tipi, bringing Patch's head up, ears on alert. His muscles bunched as he readied for a quick retreat through the slash he'd made in the side of the dwelling. Roan's hand on his ruff stopped him.

"Stay, boy, it's me friend you are, much as anyone. Me friend and me soulmate. Stay."

Still tense, Patch lay still, his eyes bright and watchful. He relaxed when Falcon and Hilton entered.

As they seated themselves, Hilton commented, "Damned if I don't believe you'll make a house pet of that wolf yet, Roan."

"Aye, but not a pet. A friend. Patch is already that, just as you are, Thax Hilton. Friends, the both of you."

Falcon looked doubtful. "He's a wild beast, Roan. Why are you making a pet, a friend of him. I should think you would want him to run free. His eyes, usually bright and mischievous, dulled with what struck Roan as inner sadness.

"You've bit into the wee problem we have there, Falcon. He isn't a wild beast, Patch isn't. True it is he has wild blood in his veins, but I'm thinking he's been around man since he was a wee *bairn*."

"Been wondering why he took up with you, Roan."

"Aye. The closer to me he stays, too — until I'm well enough to take him away again. It's me thinking the less chance he has of getting a rancher's bullet, so long as he remains in me presence."

"No doubt you're right, but didn't he roam wild long before he met up with you?"

"Aye, it's a fact, maybe two, three years."

"He's lucky then."

"Or smarter than most humans. How do your people feel about him?"

"They saw him when we brought you in."

Hilton interrupted. "Yes, and there were a good many frightened people for a few minutes, too. Falcon and his boys had to do some fast explaining."

Falcon nodded and laughed. "I never saw bows strung so fast and arrows readied. But those white patches and his size make him easily recognized. The People pay him no mind now."

Roan stroked Patch's head. "It's a good thing to know. I'll not be wanting your people afraid to move about because of Patch. I'd be leaving here meself, should that be the case."

"Hah!" Falcon laughed. "Not likely. In the first place Tula wouldn't allow it. Second, you're not well enough." He looked to Hilton for support.

Hilton took up the conversation. "Hell, man, you're so weak your legs wouldn't hold you up for five steps."

Roan grinned and propped himself up on his right arm. The effort forced beads of sweat to pop out on his forehead. "It's just possible you both be right. His breathing was labored. "It's well over a week I've lain here and it's sunshine I'll be needing. Whether me nurse likes it or not, it's sunshine I'll get. Now, would one of you fine gentlemen be for lending me a hand so's I can get to me feet?"

Falcon and Hilton exchanged glances. "Tula will have our hides nailed to the wall of Warren Quade's study," Falcon said, "but I think he's right, Hilton. Let's hurry, though, before she gets back. I'll help him outside. You grab one of those robes for him to sit on."

Taking Roan's good arm, Falcon lifted him to his feet where he stood uncertainly, his legs trembling and weak.

Hilton raised the flap of the tipi. Falcon supported most of Roan's weight as he maneuvered him through the narrow opening. Roan stood in the sun's warmth, his arm around Falcon's shoulders.

He lifted his face to the warm sunlight. With effort, he filled his lungs with fresh morning dampness and woodsmoke from the circles of fires within the village.

" 'Tis a fine day for living," he said, and readily accepted the robe Hilton spread out on the ground, easing himself down until he sat in cross-legged Indian fashion, his back straight. Beads of sweat rolled from his hairline. Exhausted from even this slight effort, Roan breathed deeply and smiled.

Patch appeared from between the tipis, surveyed the area and strolled to Roan's side where he stretched out. Roan ran his fingers through the stiff fur at the back of Patch's neck.

More relaxed now, Roan studied his surroundings. Hundreds of tipis were set up in rows, leaving aisles where four horses abreast could ride through. A plump woman in a fringed skirt and waist shirt came from the lodge across the aisle. She regarded him, her eyes widening. Suddenly, she screamed. The anguished wail echoed through the village, bringing others streaming from their tipis.

Startled, Roan gasped, "What the devil — ? Holy Mother of Jesus, what's happening?"

"You'll see," Falcon told him.

The woman chattered to the others in a high-pitched voice, all the while pointing toward Roan.

Other people came forward and gathered around. Smiles lighted their faces as they approached.

Already apprehensive, Roan became even more nervous when drums began a steady throbbing.

116

The women shuffled their feet, swayed to the beat and chanted. Roan looked to Falcon for explanation. The Indian stood with arms folded across his chest. He chuckled impishly.

"Will you stop that braying, you jackass," Roan snapped, "and be for telling me what it is they do."

Falcon nudged Hilton and nodded as they sat down by Roan.

"Damn! That *was* a little spooky," Hilton admitted. "Come on, Falcon, what was she shouting. The way they converged on us, I thought they were going to stake old Roan out on an anthill or something. I've heard stories about interesting punishments your people have developed."

Still chuckling, Falcon said, "Not Roan, not our adopted brother. He's one of us now. The woman was telling the others that Tac-se-nas is well, for all of them to come and see. Now they thank *Wakan Tanka* for the life of a brother."

Without missing a shuffle, the dancers parted in the middle. Through that opening moved a magnificent figure. A blanket covered his tall frame. His broad shoulders and his back remained ramrod straight. Over his head was a hood bearing the horns of a buffalo, curving outward then upward at the tips. The curved beak of a gigantic bird protruded over his weathered face.

"It's Oien-Ta," Falcon said. "He'll be speaking

our tongue today, but I'll try to interpret for you. Whatever you do, my friends, don't object to his words or actions."

Patch growled low in his throat and backed away from the costumed Shaman. The wolf settled on his haunches near the back of the tipi.

The drums silenced and the dance halted as the old medicine man stopped in front of Roan. His gnarled hand moved out from beneath the blanket. Bending, he raised the bandage on Roan's shoulder roughly. Roan winced and clenched his teeth against the pain.

Oien-Ta studied the wound, surprise mirrored in his black eyes. He released the bandage and stepped back a couple of paces. *"Wash-ta!"* he shouted.

"Very good," Falcon interpreted.

With a dramatic flair, Oien-Ta removed the blanket from around him, revealing the shining black feathered wings attached to his arms. He stepped forward again, wrapping the blanket around Roan. Retreating, he straightened and looked toward the heavens, arms extended. Slowly, he turned in a circle, mournful words flowing from his throat.

"Hos-toc Wakanda es-Mori-has-tan Tac-se-nas."

Falcon leaned toward Hilton and Roan. "He thanks the spirit of the four winds for the life of The People's brother."

This time, the aged Shaman moved his winged arms backward and forward gracefully. *"Hos-tae Wakanda ke-sol-ke lumoe has-tan Tac-se-nas."*

118

"This time he thanks the spirits of the sun and moon."

Roan found himself increasingly bored as the chant droned on. Oien-Ta thanked the spirits of the trees, the grass, and a good many other entities for the gifts Wakan Tanka had given The People.

When he mentioned the strong medicine of horse dung, Falcon had to shush his companions. Roan struggled to hide the mirth that tugged at him. He was afraid to look at Hilton, fearing the two of them would burst forth into laughter and embarrass Falcon.

The Shaman continued, thanking the myriad *Wakandas.* Suddenly, he jumped backward then leaped high into the air. The drums again throbbed to life, keeping time with the hopping, skipping dance around the circle of those gathered to watch.

Roan studied his garb. Small gourds, strung on rawhide, encircled his ankles, keeping time with the pace of the dance.

"He has to be old," Hilton whispered. "But the deep lines of age don't go with the way he can dance around."

Falcon smiled. "He's well into his seventieth summer."

Oien-Ta's voice rose in a strong, powerful chant.

"Now he is praising himself. He says Wakan Tanka gave him all these powers, the power to cure Tac-se-nas."

"Here now, let's be for praising the right people," Roan objected, keeping his voice low. "It was Tula who —"

"Sh-h-h, let him finish. He says he performed a miracle this time. There will be no missing flesh, no deep holes in the body of Tac-se-nas, our brother. There will be only small scars reminding our brother of the great medicine given to him by Wakan Tanka through his servant Oien-Ta. There will be no crippling in the limbs. Our brother will be as good as he was before, all because Oien-Ta has this great power."

After the praises were repeated several times to make certain each person knew of his greatness, the medicine man quieted. Before Roan, he spread the winged arms and fluttered them.

"Waugh!" he said, barely out of breath. With steady gait, he walked through the crowd which separated to allow him passage.

The people dispersed into their lodges.

Angrily, Roan turned to Falcon. "Oien-Ta's magic, is it? Why, by all that's holy, does the old rascal say these things? Is he daft? Tula Moon deserves the credit and it's to her I'll be giving me thanks."

Hilton agreed. "I think so, too."

"Maybe what you say is true." Falcon shrugged. "Would one of you like to tell Oien-Ta that? I'll not do it nor will Tula."

"And, by Jesus, why not?"

"Because," Falcon said with a sigh, "you don't tell the second highest, and sometimes the high-

120

est, power in the tribe that his power is not so great." He leaned back, supporting himself on his hands, and looked skyward. "Besides, even though the missionary school taught against some of our cultural beliefs, I still think the Shaman has mystic powers."

"Why so?" Hilton asked.

"When I was a boy, not more than ten or eleven summers, Oien-Ta brought a dead man to life."

"Only one person I ever heard of that did that," Hilton grumbled. "And his name wasn't Oien-Ta. It was Jesus."

"Aye," Roan said. "You wouldn't be telling us the likes of Oien-Ta is another Christ, would you?"

"Not at all," Falcon answered, an edge of irritation in his tone. "I, too, was taught the white man's faith, but I tell you I saw this man. He was coated with blood. Dead. Our village was down in Tongue River country then. The men had been hunting buffalo and the herd stampeded. Two great bulls charged this brave's horse. The horse went down and the man was trampled by the herd."

"Damn!" Hilton exclaimed.

Falcon gave him a sharp look. The Indian's eyes glistened with a mixture of excitement and sorrow. "The others brought him into camp in late evening. They said he was dead, but Oien-Ta used his powers. Two days later, this man walked to his own lodge. He lived two more years and died bravely in a battle with the yellow-legged pony soldiers."

"And you're wanting us to believe you saw the old man do this?" Roan asked.

"Believe it or not," Falcon snapped. He drew himself to his feet and stared into the distance, looking back into a memory that obviously disturbed him. "The man's name was White Eagle. He was my father."

He turned and walked away.

Roan watched Falcon's broad back until the young Indian turned between the tipis and disappeared from view.

"Damn," Hilton said, shaking his head, "his father."

"Aye, friend, I'm thinking we put our feet in a wide puddle that time."

"Too bad we didn't stick them in our mouths *before* we spoke."

"By the blood of me sainted mother, I'll have more respect for Oien-Ta from this day on."

"Do you think maybe Falcon deserves an apology?"

Roan nodded. "Aye, and it's one he'll be getting."

Chapter Ten

Roan expected daily visits from Hilton and Falcon. The day after Oien-Ta's prayer ceremony, they didn't come. He grew more restless with each hour that passed.

At noon, he asked Tula, "Where do you suppose me friends have got off to this fine day?"

Her back to him, she stirred the cooking pot and kept silent.

"Tula, me girl, what is it? What's wrong?"

She turned slowly. One look at her face was enough. Her words only added credence to what he already feared. "Falcon and Hilton were arrested last night."

Roan laughed. "Saints be, you had me half expecting something terrible. Soon they'll learn they can't keep Falcon on the reservation."

"Roan." Tula gripped his shoulders. "Promise me you won't upset yourself if I tell you the rest."

"Tell me, but it'll be no promises I give until I hear."

"The reservation guards are working on it now. But Hilton and Falcon are in the jail in Buckhorn."

"For what?"

"Jake Tanner caught them poaching on Steppe's ranch."

"I'll not be believing such nonsense. Neither of them would set a foot on the Double S and it's that I'll swear to." He pushed her hands away and struggled to his feet. The effort resulted in searing pain in his side. Sweat beaded on his forehead and upper lip. "I'll not believe a word of it until I hear it from their own mouths."

"There's nothing you can do. You'll have your wounds open and bleeding again, Roan. Let the authorities take care of it."

"It's me Jake Tanner's after and it's me friends he'll go through to get me."

"It had nothing to do with you. Tanner found them with a deer they'd shot — on Steppe's property."

Roan's legs gave. He crumpled to a heap on the floor of the tipi. " 'Tis a sorry man I am, Tula Moon, that I've got not enough strength to help me friends." His breath came in gasps. He tried to rise again and failed, sinking back onto the hides. Tears stung his eyes. "Will you do this for me? Will you find out now if Hilton and Falcon are all right?"

"I'll talk to the reservation police. You rest now. Promise you'll stay quiet."

"I'll promise you. You go now."

He slept a little during her absence, a restless slumber, filled with nightmares.

Faces swirled around him — faces with evil smiles painted in garish colors.

From the midst of the faces came the sound of insane laughter, taunting the figure in the center of the tightly drawn circle of dark forms.

He floated above the scene. The dancing ring of

evil spun faster, faster around the solitary gray crea-
ture, threatening him with gestures of violence.

Slowly, he descended until he could see the bris-
tling hairs on the creature's back, hear the low,
menacing growl.

Fire spewed from his hands as he hung, suspended,
fire burning the men in black wings, undulating wings
moving ever closer to the lone wolf.

She stepped through the brightness at the opening
of the circle — lovely, tawny — and called his name.
The word was like wind soughing through the pine
grove. "Roan."

He tried to speak, but had no voice.

"Roan," she persisted. "Roan! Wake up!"

Still groggy, he tried to focus on Tula, returned
from her visit to the reservation guard. "Are me
friends all right?" he asked, trying to shake off
the dream.

"They say the marshal won't release Falcon to
them. And they have no authority over Hilton."

"I thought it was the law Indians had to be
tried by their own."

Tula shook her head. "Roan, when has the
white man's law ever served The People fairly?"

"Then what of Hilton and Falcon? What's to
be done?"

"They've already had them before a judge. Jake
Tanner testified against them."

"And — ?"

"The judge sentenced them to hang tomorrow
morning."

He moaned. "And no chance to speak to them."

"The guards were able to see them — for only a minute or two. Hilton says they were still on the reservation, that Tanner forced them to Steppe's land at gunpoint."

"He's as rotten as the bog moss, Tula Moon, that one is. I'll be going after me friends at dusk."

"You're going nowhere. You have to promise. Falcon is of my blood. I don't want him to die, but neither do I want you dead. You must promise."

Roan brushed a strand of hair back from her face. "I'll be making no promises to be broken."

Night slid over the reservation pulling a blanket of moonlight with it.

Roan cursed the brightness as he raised himself on one elbow and looked across the tipi at Tula's sleeping form. Her back turned to him, she breathed so softly he wondered if she breathed at all.

He threw off the heavy buffalo robe that covered him and forced himself to rise, holding fast to one of the poles to steady himself. Dizziness washed over him as he staggered to the tipi entrance. He groped near the entry for his rifle. Damned if he hadn't seen it leaning there just this day.

His fingers closed around the sturdy wooden butt. He hefted it so the barrel rested across his good arm.

Tula stirred, rolled onto her back.

He held his breath, waiting, listening for her

quiet, even breathing to continue. When it did, he pushed aside the flap and stumbled through to the cool night air.

The burning in his side increased. He put his hand to the bandages and felt the sticky warmth of blood. "If it's me lot to die, then let it be," he whispered. "I'll not let the likes of Jake Tanner get away with his skullduggery."

The horses grazed in the lea behind the tipi. Roan hurried his pace, found it to be a mistake. Time and again, his legs collapsed and he thudded to the ground.

He whistled softly for the dun, waited until it trotted from amid the Indian ponies. He had neither time nor strength to saddle the animal, but the two of them had learned each other's ways in the past months. Roan gathered all his strength, clambered onto the horse's broad back, grasped his coarse mane and clicked the order to run, urging with his boot heels.

The air rushing past revived him. He slowed the dun to a lope. It would be five hours at the least before he reached Buckhorn. If he bled to death, if the horse dropped dead under him, Hilton and Falcon would die, too.

He rested the rifle across the animal's back and forced himself to relax. He awakened with a start hours later and realized he rode along Dalhart Street, the main thoroughfare of Buckhorn.

The jail, a crude log structure, stood near the end of the street. The marshal — or one of the locals he'd paid — would stay in the office as long as a prisoner was in the cell. In his condition, Roan couldn't handle a face-to-face confrontation. He had to think of some diversion.

His side throbbed. He touched his blood-soaked shirt, groaned and fought the wave of nausea that washed over him. If only he could find a way to quench the fire of pain.

Fire. That was the answer. A fire would draw out whoever was in the jail. He studied the buildings around him, his gaze falling on a ramshackle shed back of the livery.

He stumbled into the thicket behind the shed and grasped hands full of dried grass. Piling it near the rear wall, he slipped a match from his watch pocket and dragged it across the rough fabric of his trousers.

Like tinder, the grass blazed. Like damp wood, it smoked and fizzled into dead embers.

He tried again, watching the growing line of rose along the horizon. Dawn, if it came before he got to the jail, would defeat him.

Three times more he set the flame. On the third, the aging wood of the back wall caught. Fire crawled up two of the boards, spreading to the sides as it climbed.

Within minutes, the blaze lighted the area around. Roan fired his rifle into the air and urged the dun into the alley behind the buildings.

A woman appeared in an upstairs window across from the livery. "Fire!" she screamed. "Fire!"

Roan waited until the street filled with people,

one of them the marshal.

Certain it was safe to head for the jail, he kneed the horse into a walk and tried to relax his tensed muscles.

A single lamp, turned low, glowed from the desk inside the office. The keys to the cells hung on a ring inside the entrance. Roan lifted them from their holders and made his way to the door leading to the barred cubicles.

Hilton snored loud enough. Roan heard the sounds before he entered the cell block.

Falcon lay on the floor, a thin blanket pulled to his waist. Quiet, even breathing convinced Roan that he, too, slept.

"Falcon," he whispered, then louder, "Falcon Claw."

Hilton muttered something unintelligible and rolled onto his side.

"Falcon," Roan said aloud. His voice echoed in the stillness now that Hilton had stopped snoring.

Falcon sat up. In the dim light coming through the high, barred window in back of the cell, Roan could see the young Indian's bright eyes searching for the source of what had awakened him.

"It's me, friend Falcon, Roan McCrae. Wake Mister Hilton there, quietly as you can."

"Roan?" Falcon said. "What is it? What's going on?"

"I've come to take you out of this place. We'll find a safe hiding place until we can all go north."

He fitted the key into the lock and turned it.

The tumblers clanked loudly. The door swung wide.

Hilton took no time waking from sleep. A gunfighter, he told Roan once, slept with his mind constantly alert. Otherwise, he explained, he would die.

He stood, took one step toward freedom and stopped short, shoulders squared, hand ready at his side even though he had no weapon.

"What in hell are you doing here, McCrae?" he asked. "Are you trying to kill yourself? You're not ready for this sort of thing."

"You'll be kind enough to let me worry about meself, Mister Hilton, and you'll come along without —"

The unmistakable click of a revolver being cocked stopped him in mid-sentence.

He whirled, his rifle ready.

"I figured you'd try to pull something like this, mick," Jake Tanner said. "That's why I talked the marshal into letting me sleep in the other cell tonight. Surprised?"

Roan's finger tightened on the trigger.

"I wouldn't think about pulling that if I was you," Tanner warned.

"And what is it you'll be doing besides dying if I do?"

"Well, mick, I'll tell you. You pull that trigger, I'll pull mine and the Injun there's gonna have a hole right where his left eye is."

"You filthy sonofa—" The burning in Roan's side hit with a fury. Whatever he intended to do, he had to do it now. He lunged. At the same time, he flipped the rifle until he gripped it by the barrel.

He swung wildly. The butt connected with Tanner's shoulder, bringing an oath.

A shot echoed through the room.

Roan had time to call, "Falcon —" but fire, white hot, seared through his head.

He groaned once, clutched at his head and dropped to the floor.

Chapter Eleven

Acrid smoke burned his nostrils. No longer was Patch centered in the circle of dark dancers. Instead, Roan hunched there, pain racking his body and fear tearing at his soul.

Black wings beat a harsh rhythm above him. Not the wings of Oien-Ta's medicine, but wings of a bird of prey, talons clutching at Roan's head, sharp beak peeling bits of flesh from his torn side.

No cool breeze penetrated the evil to soothe him. The dancers revolved around him, chanting, "Death. Death. Death."

One, tall and muscular, broke from the circle and moved in on him, jabbing him with a long, pointed stick, prodding his wounds, making them raw and full of misery.

"Die," ordered the gruff-voiced figure. "Die, you mick bastard."

Die! The word echoed over and over like the tolling of a huge bell in the distance, sounding the knell for the life of a single unwanted soul.

"Die," another voice joined the chant — softer, gentler. No, the word the second voice spoke wasn't "die." Something else.

"Don't die." That was it. The second, the gentle voice was urging him to disobey the devil dancer, the one who looked like Jake Tanner.

"Don't die, Roan. Stay with us."

He opened his eyes, wondering how he could

have watched the death dance with them closed.

Beauty in the face above him convinced him he had died and gone to heaven. Except that his Da always said there was no pain in heaven and his head and side were filled with pain.

"Be it Heaven or Hell I've been sent to?" he murmured.

"Neither, Roan McCrae, just the reservation," Tula said in her husky tone. "And more of Oien-Ta's treatment."

"And how much of me brain did Jake Tanner's weapon rob from me?"

"It never touched your brain, Roan. Only nicked you — just above the ear, but if you ever do something like this again and Tanner doesn't kill you, I might."

"Ah, fair Tula, are you telling me you were worried about me?"

"You came nearer bleeding to death than you did dying from Tanner's shot. When they brought you in here and I saw those bandages, covered with blood, I was sure —"

"And me friends, Falcon and Hilton? Are they safe?"

"Thanks to a fool," Thax Hilton answered, his black face gleaming in the dim light of the tipi. "Just what did you think you were doing, Roan? Did you think Falcon and I were too stupid to get ourselves out?"

" 'Twasn't stupidity I considered, me friend. 'Twas the conniving of that rapscallion, Jake Tanner. Did I kill him, by any chance?"

133

"You didn't even touch him, but you kept him busy long enough for the two of us to shove him in the cell and lock the door."

"Then the two of you are wanted men and what in the name of all saints are you doing here? It's hiding you should be."

Hilton shook his head. "Azle Steppe's decided Tanner might have been mistaken when he said we were on Double S land."

"That's mighty charitable of him."

"I think Mister Steppe doesn't want to deal with the entire tribe if Falcon Claw is hanged. A visit from Warren Quade persuaded him such a possibility existed and he would be well advised to take another road."

"Then you'll both be in fine fettle as will I." Roan smiled and grasped Hilton's hand.

Hilton's smile faded. "Roan, you'd be smart to use caution where Tanner is concerned. You've bested him each time you've met."

"Aye, and I'll wager he'll not be coming around for another dose."

"He's a dangerous man. He'll be out for vengeance because you've shamed him. My word of advice would be to watch your back."

Roan shrugged off the warning, but well he knew how right Thax Hilton was. "Where might Falcon be?" he asked.

"Hunting with the young men," Hilton said. "Where did you suppose?"

"After all that happened last night, I thought —"

"Last night?"

"Aye, with Tanner and all, I thought —"

"Roan," Tula said, "it was three days ago. Falcon waited to thank you, but when you hadn't awakened this morning, he decided to go hunting . . . on Q-C land, with Warren's permission."

A spasm of pain rumbled like thunder through Roan's head. He leaned back and accepted the offering of sleep that swept over him.

Days of sunshine sped Roan's healing process. He could move about without help — at least from his pallet to a chair outside. Crudely fashioned from logs lashed together with rawhide, the chair was a gift from Thax Hilton. The back of the chair, covered by soft buffalo hide, gave Roan a semblance of comfort as he relaxed during the daylight hours.

It wasn't just the warming rays, though, that brought about the swift healing of his wounds. The women in the tribe made his needs a priority. They competed with each other in bringing tasty food — roast venison, wild grouse, berries, pears, persimmons.

One jolly old squaw — Falcon called her *Aka-ta-no*, Woman-Who-Screams-Like-The-Hawk, a name well-earned considering the way she shrieked that first day when Roan appeared outside the tipi — brought him a gourd full of honey and fresh corn cakes which she called *gos-kema*. Through her careful instructions, most of which were done in frantic gestures, since she spoke little English, he learned to soak the *gos-kema* in

135

the honey. With a toothless grin, she left him, the empty honey gourd clutched in her hand.

Renewed in both spirit and health, Roan relaxed and enjoyed goodwill toward the people of the village. But the idyllic existence couldn't last and he damn well knew it.

He sat in the sun as usual that morning, watching Tula's graceful movements as she walked toward him. His heart ached. Like a spectre of doom, truth loomed over him. She would speak of goodbye, not because she wanted to hurt him, but because she *must* speak of it. It, like her obligation to Warren Quade, was the way of The People.

She strode with purpose in the typical straight-toed Indian way. Most of the Sioux, he had observed, walked in the same manner, straight and proud.

God, she was beautiful. The aching in his heart increased to an unmerciful throbbing as she approached. He loved her and there wasn't any way to control the depth of his feelings. Her words tumbled through his memory. "We will never speak of this again."

He *had* to speak of it, had to tell her how he felt.

Closer now, her face was set in a sad expression. He wanted to bolt, to run into the woods and hide, hoping if she couldn't find him to tell him goodbye, the goodbye would never come.

Tears stung his eyes. He blinked them back, unwilling to let his stoic Indian friends see the weak-willed Irishman cry. If only they knew how much he had cried. He wept when Katie was killed and for two years after that. Now, the tears were for another lost love, a love that must stand back because of Tula's devotion to the ways of her people.

As she approached, he studied her lithe movements, committing them to memory, knowing full well his memories would be all she would leave him with.

In one hand, she carried a folded piece of cloth. The other held a pair of scissors, borrowed no doubt from the white man's infirmary. Deftly, she snipped them a couple of times as she stopped in front of him.

"You are looking shaggy, my friend Roan. I think we'd better give you a haircut. And, if you like, I'll even trim up that red wool that covers your face." She wrapped the cloth around his shoulders and moved behind him.

"If you've a mind to cut me mane, fair Tula, then do it, but you'll do no more than give me beard a trim. When the weather heats up, I'll be shaving it off I suppose, though for the life of me I don't know why. Appearance means nothing to a man alone."

Tula, who had already begun trimming the wiry hair on the back of his head, stopped. She stepped in front of him, a stern look on her face. "Are we feeling sorry for ourselves this morning?" She wrapped her fingers in his beard and gently lifted his head so she could peer into his eyes.

"If we are, that's one thing, Roan McCrae, but let's not be telling ourselves lies."

"Lies, is it? And what would be the falsehood I've told?"

"Pride in a man has nothing to do with being alone. And inside or out, Roan, you run over the brim with pride."

Without further chastisement, she resumed her barbering. Silence, uncomfortable and heavy, hung over them.

As she moved around to trim his ragged beard, he finally broke the silence. "I suppose you'll be leaving me today."

For several moments, she said nothing. The hand holding the scissors trembled.

"You'll not be answering me, Tula Moon?" he asked.

The intense effort strained her voice as she strove to keep it hard and steady. "Yes. I'll be leaving the reservation in a few minutes. You're well enough to get by now. You don't need me."

With precision, she cropped his moustache close, keeping her eyes averted from his.

He studied her loveliness. She bit her lower lip. Their gazes met, briefly. The black pools of her eyes filled to the brim with tears that escaped and rolled down her smooth cheeks.

The scissors stopped clacking. She whirled and stepped away, turning back to say, in words barely audible, "Goodbye, heart-that-beats-within-me."

Roan, despite the tenderness of his healing

wounds, threw the blanket from his lap and rose from the chair. He seized her wrist in his callused hand. "Just a minute, me love." He pulled her toward the entrance to the tipi.

"No, Roan," she protested.

He forced her inside the dwelling, ignoring the pain shooting through his left arm. He held her close.

Her arms clasped around him as she wept. All he could do for several seconds was hold her as he struggled to find his voice.

"Tula, me love, I heard you when you said love wasn't to be spoken of again, but before you go, girl, you have to know this. 'Tis you I hold, not me Katie. You're seeing me in me right mind and I'm saying to you I love you, Tula Moon."

"Don't!" she cried.

Roan captured her lips and found them warm and soft as they responded. He wished beyond any prayer he had ever uttered to the saints that the kiss could last forever. But his bliss was too brief. She pulled away and stepped back from him.

"Remember our promise, my heart," she reminded. "Goodbye now." Without another word or glance, she walked away, leaving him staring at the barren tipi.

Stepping outside, he studied her retreating form running down the wide aisle between the rows of tipis. He kept her in his sight, filled his memory with her until she moved out of his vision and darted between two of the lodges far ahead.

Exhaustion overwhelmed him. He moved out of the bright sunshine into the dimness of the tipi. He lay down on the pallet and stared at the smoke hole in the top without seeing it. How could he stop the turmoil that boiled through his mind? Hardly aware he had done it, he shouted, "Damn you, Warren Quade!"

Immediately, he wished he could retract the words. He thought of how Tula had said, "Warren Quade is your friend. To wish his death would be my ruin and yours."

Yes, Warren Quade was his friend and one of very few, so why did he so fervently wish Quade wasn't a friend? He sighed and realized all he wanted to do at the moment was to find Patch and head toward the North Territory. Common sense and the lack of strength in his muscles, too long without exercise, kept him there. "All right, Roan McCrae," he told himself, "so you're not so well yet. Two weeks and you will be. Two weeks, it is and you'll be gone from the heartache."

He lay back against the soft hides and closed his eyes.

Thax Hilton whispering his name awakened him. Thax squatted next to him, peering intently at Roan's face. "You all right," he asked.

"Aye, as all right as a man who's dying can be, I guess."

"Dying? Roan, are your wounds giving you

trouble? If they are —"

"Nay, not me wounds, friend Hilton. It's me heart and there ain't no mending to be done to it." He sighed deeply. "Where's Falcon?"

"He and his boys went hunting last night. Tula didn't tell you?"

"She only told me she'd be leaving today."

"I know about that." Hilton hesitated, his expression stating plainly he had more to say and wasn't keen about saying it.

"Spit it out, me friend. What's chewing at your insides?"

"I'm going with her, Roan."

"And why would you be doing that?"

"I think they'll need my services at the Q-C. Azle Steppe has big plans, plans that will call for gunfighters. Warren Quade may be needing his own firearms experts."

Roan nodded. "Aye. I'll be hoping Quade has the good sense to realize that and hire you." He made an effort to get to his feet.

Hilton wrapped an arm around him for support, but Roan shook it off. "I'll be standing on me own," he told Hilton. "If I allow the lot of you to do these things for me, I'll never get me strength back and get away from this place."

Hilton's brows arched in a questioning expression. "What are your plans, Roan? Are you going after Jake Tanner? You got in mind to get even for them burning your place?"

"Aye, that, too, but not just yet. I'll be taking meself far north to take Patch away from Tanner's hungry gunsights. That was me plan when the grizzly found me and it's still me intention."

Hilton ran a thumb across his chin thoughtfully. "Yes, Falcon told me. Well —" He held forth his hand. "So long, my friend. If things heat up before you return. I'll do my best to take care of Tanner in your name."

Feeling still another fleeting sense of loss, Roan gripped Hilton's hand. "You do that for me, Mister Hilton, and you take with you me thanks for your friendship. I have nothing but faith that you'll know how to tackle anything facing you. Watch your back as well."

"I'll remember, Roan. *Hasta luego,* my friend." Hilton turned away.

"Sure and *hasta luego* to yourself — whatever that means."

Hilton said over his shoulder, "It's Spanish. It means 'until later.' "

"Aye," Roan answered, not feeling at all sure he would ever see anyone again. At that moment, loneliness, enough to cover the whole blessed universe, enveloped him.

Desolation hung over Roan like a shroud. For five days that stretched into what seemed like a year, Roan awaited Falcon's return. When the jovial Indian came into camp, he stopped by to pass only a few moments. As soon as he went about his own business, the devastating loneliness returned.

Roan had never been one to think of being

142

alone. Even back in Ireland, when he was younger, he had been a man who liked solitude. Roaming the rolling green hills of the Old Sod or walking along the seashore or marshes, he preferred to be alone. Maybe now the awful emptiness was a result of his injuries, a sickness born of them. He had never known illness or serious injury. That had to be the answer. His wounds kept him confined.

As it always did in moments of discomfort, his mind drifted to Katie. The days after her death had been fraught with the same kind of loneliness, but not constantly, not like now. Then, he kept busy, hunting wolves or brawling in the saloons which left no time to dwell on misery.

Never had he known this kind of devastation. The first week or so, when the fever was upon him, he thought of nothing but getting well. Tula, Falcon, Hilton, even Patch, constantly hovered near him, concerned for his welfare

Patch. Where *was* that scoundrel? The great beast had been absent all day. Perhaps he accepted Falcon's thoughtfulness now that Roan no longer needed his constant watchfulness. When they brought Roan to the village, Falcon placed him in this particular tipi because it was the last in the row. Only open field spread out behind it.

"It will give your Wolf friend freedom to come and go without nearing the other lodges," he said.

Roan got up from the chair and sauntered to

the rear of the tipi, staring out across the expanse of the field. At the back of the flat lea stood a line of tall lodge pole pines, maybe a quarter mile distant. On impulse, Roan strolled toward them. He needed the exercise and, as long as he took it slow and easy, the walk would do him no harm.

He made it to the brake without difficulty. Leaning against the trunk of one of the pines, he peered into the forest's dimness, listening to the peaceful quiet which surrounded him. Only the chittering of a squirrel and the distant cawing of a crow disturbed the silence.

He ventured into the glade. In another meadow area beyond the trees, a flash of movement caught his eye. Cautiously, he moved forward to sate his curiosity. Stepping carefully, keeping hidden behind the tree trunks, his patience was rewarded. Patch lay at the edge of the copse and basked in the warm sunlight.

A smaller wolf in a prone position laid beside him.

Eager for a closer look, Roan took another step. Beneath his foot a twig snapped, shattering the stillness.

Instantly, Patch and his companion were up and running. With the motion, the smaller wolf's belly hung low. A bitch — with pups! Patch's pups? But how could that be?

Striding into the clearing, Roan covered a few more paces. He whistled for Patch.

More than halfway across the lea now, Patch halted and turned his head. The she-wolf disappeared into another copse of trees.

"Come, Patch," Roan ordered with a snap of his fingers.

Patch stood, looking uncertainly from Roan to the spot where his mate had disappeared. Finally, he trotted to Roan's side.

He held the big wolf's head in his hands and stroked the stiff hair. "So you've found yourself a mate, have you now, me boy? She's a beauty, she is. But I don't understand how it can be you've got a family already. It's only three weeks ago we came here. Would you kindly be for explaining the situation to me?"

A wolf mated for life. Of that, he was certain. Yet here was a bitch with whelps that couldn't possibly belong to Patch. Unless —

He threw back his head and laughed. Bubbling from within him, the laughter felt good.

"You sly devil, you. Your mate's been with us all along, ain't she? And meself thinking I was a wolfer. By the saints, me friend, never one time did I see her. Aye, and she's one to be proud of."

Roan glanced toward the copse. The she-wolf stood, half-hidden by the trees, watching them. "And what should we be calling her? A beauty such as she needs a name to be proud of. Let's call her Shadow since she kept herself secreted from me until this day. Aye, Shadow she be."

Patch twitched his ears as if to say he understood — and approved.

"She'll be needing you, Patch, me boy. Go on.

Go to her. We'll be leaving these parts soon, you and me and your family. Go now, but come see me in the morning so I won't be concerning meself with your safety. Go."

Patch licked Roan's hand and whined. Quickly, he turned and ran toward his mate.

Roan smiled. As he returned to the lodge, he noted with a thanks to the Holy Mother that the lonely ache had found a niche somewhere to slide into.

Chapter Twelve

Roan had to find the wolf's lair. He went to the clearing where he had seen Patch and his mate. From there, he walked in a wide circle, decreasing the diameter with each turn. By the third round, he noticed a downed tree with high grass growing around it. Strands of hair clung to the dead branches.

Wolf's hair, for sure.

He moved closer. Shadow did not trust him like Patch did. Too much of his scent and she would move the pups. He wanted her to see him and Patch together, to learn he could be her friend.

Moving some fifty yards, Roan gathered tree limbs. He had to fashion some sort of cage to carry Shadow and her pups. It would be well to build it where she could watch.

His labors had just begun when Patch came to investigate. Roan, busy trimming limbs off a fallen tree, took time to give Patch's head a couple of pats and to run his fingers through the wolf's ruff. "Sit, boy. Sit and keep me company."

Patch stretched out in the sunshine.

"Now we'll be seeing what that lady of yours will do." He glanced toward the lair. Shadow, keeping low to the ground, slunk inside the den.

Twice in the next three hours; she lifted her head above the brush and thick grass to study the activities between Roan and Patch.

In late evening, Roan finished trimming the last limb. He gave Patch one last affectionate pat and stood, rubbing the aching muscles in his back. "Tomorrow, me boy, we'll be building the cage. You go see to your family now."

A glance over his shoulder assured him Patch trotted eagerly toward his mate.

With first light of morning, Roan paced anxiously in front of the tipi. He had work to do, the cage to finish. Jake Tanner and Azle Steppe wouldn't wait forever to seek their vengeance and Patch had come to mean more and more to Roan as the days passed. Had he examined the deepest feelings inside him, he might have discovered that the wolf was a balm covering the intensity of his losses — first Katie, now Tula Moon.

Wanting to be about the work waiting there, he darted quick glances toward the clearing in back of the tipi, but after the scolding he had received the previous evening from the Indian women, he was afraid to be seen sneaking out.

Their exaggerated hand gestures and frantic voices told him, despite the fact he didn't understand their language, that they thought he had left without saying a proper farewell. Finally, their frowns metamorphosed into smiles and they stuffed him with good food.

Now, this morning, he would wait until they brought breakfast to avoid a recurrence of the scene.

Instead of the women, though, he was visited by Oien-Ta, the shaman.

148

Roan rose to his feet and nodded in greeting.

Returning the nod brusquely, the old man examined Roan's healing wounds. "Wash-ta," he said. "You leave soon, hah?"

"Aye, soon it is."

"You take wolf brother to north in two suns?"

Roan nodded. "But how is it you know? Did me friend Falcon — ?"

The shaman spread his hands. "Wakondas know all, tell Oien-Ta Tac-se-nas leave soon." He placed his hand on Roan's shoulder. "Tac-se-nas brother to People now. Return soon."

Roan laid his own hand over the aged one. "It'll be me pleasure, Oien-Ta. Your people be me own and I'm beholden to you. It's certain I'll be back one day."

"Waugh." The old man pushed aside the flap of the tipi and left.

No sooner had he departed than the women came, smiling and offering more than enough smoked venison, corn cakes and honey to last him through the day. He ate his fill and wrapped the rest in one of the grease-soaked cloths. "I'll be gone from you most of this day, me friends. This'll keep a body from starving during his labors. It's me thanks you have, the lot of you."

When cut into long strips, one of the fur robes which made up his pallet inside the tipi worked perfectly for binding together limbs that formed the cage bars.

By late afternoon, the hinges were placed for the door.

Patch watched intently.

"You see this door, me friend?" Roan said. "I'll be propping this open with that pole there." He pointed toward a length of tree limb he had trimmed for his purpose.

Patch listened, his head cocked, his ears pointed. An answering whine escaped his mouth.

"Good, it's fine you understand, old son. Now look at this. I'll be placing your pups in the back of the cage. They'll lure your mate inside. She'll trip the stick and this door will close. Then we'll tie it shut and it's on our way north, we'll be. 'Tis truly a shame we have to cage your family, me boy, but you do be understanding that, don't you?"

Patch sniffed at the structure and examined each inch of it. Finally, he settled onto the grass as though saying, "I don't see anything wrong with it."

Roan selected two long poles and lashed them to the cage. "Now, Patch me boy, we got a travois that'll be carrying your lady and your children along behind us. Would you be giving that your blessing as well?"

Patch once again inspected the workmanship and approved.

" 'Tis from here on me job gets devilish hard, friend Patch." He lifted the ends of the travois poles and dragged the cage toward the lair. " 'Tis best you come along with me. She'll not like me getting so close. Your chore will be to keep her off me until I've got this trap in place."

Patch trotted in front of him and stood at attention near the fallen tree.

Shadow crept out into the light, her fangs bared. A low growl rumbled in her throat. She lunged, leaping across the distance straight for Roan.

He sought a nearby tree to climb, should it be necessary.

Suddenly, Shadow stopped, some twenty feet away. There, she paced back and forth, the hair on her back bristling menacingly. Her growl heightened, punctuated by sharp snaps of her jaws.

Slowly, Roan edged forward dragging the cage. With each step he took, Shadow grew more excited.

Without warning, she rushed, pounding toward Roan. Her eyes spurted darts of fury.

"Patch!" he called.

Patch responded, bounding across the grassy ground. Big as Patch was, Roan wasn't at all sure he could match Shadow's need to protect her brood.

She met Patch head on, forced him to back away. Once. Twice. Three times.

Again he leaped toward her. She faced him, snarling, a wild thing fighting fiercely for her children. Patch struck at her with one massive paw.

With a yelp, she retreated, but only for a moment. Whirling, she vaulted toward Roan, who had managed to draw the cage still closer.

Patch butted her in the side, knocking her to the ground. He closed his teeth over her lower jaw and clung to the hair on her chin.

"Good, me boy," Roan called. "She can't be hurting either of us with that kind of hold."

Nervous sweat poured from Roan's body. He was as close to the she-wolf as he cared to be. He dropped the cage, effected a hasty escape to a safe distance and whistled.

Patch instantly released Shadow, approached the cage and dropped to his haunches, his long tongue lolling from the side of his mouth as he panted from exertion. He kept his gaze fastened on his mate.

With the hair along her back bristling, Shadow continued her low-throated growl and made sweeping circles around the outer perimeter of the cage, pausing occasionally to sniff at the bindings and snarl her displeasure.

"You'll have to get used to it, me girl," Roan whispered. "Starting on the morrow, it'll be your home for a few days."

He strode back to the lodge in time for the evening meal.

As the women crowded around in their usual way, he told them, "I'll be leaving in the morning."

Waves of protest arose from the gathering.

"Look, me friends," he said, laughing, "it's your own fault I'll be saying me goodbyes. Staying here will bring me to me own ruin what with the good cooks you are. Should I stay and eat what you bring me, I'll grow fat and lazy, so I'll be bidding you goodbye and I'll return once in a while for a dose of your hospitality."

Sad faces lighted with his good humor. The women joined him in laughter.

The fat matron who usually spoke for the group echoed the words of Oien-Ta. "You are our brother, Roan McCrae. You will be welcome always in our lodge."

Roan leaned against the soft robes over the chair back and closed his eyes. Tula Moon had brought him this acceptance into the hearts of her people. How good it was to be part of a family, to be in the midst of friends.

But Tula's memory haunted him. He tried to think of other things — the coming morning, how he would capture Shadow, the beauty of the northland.

Like every other time, his memories refused to be banished. He had no future, no meaning without Tula. He told Hilton as much when Hilton asked if he intended to come back and take his vengeance on Jake Tanner.

"Why bother?" he asked. "Should a man kill another, maybe two others, over a piece of land that has no meaning now?"

"But your wife's grave —"

"Katie's dear soul rests with the saints. There's nothing but dust beneath the sod." Hilton might not have understood his words, but, saints be, he wasn't certain he understood them himself. Too many times he tried to think of Katie only to find her lovely face replaced by Tula's.

Katie's lilting Irish brogue more often than not turned to the husky tones of Tula's voice. And Tula's words were those that tore at his heart, "*Wakanda da-yo.* You are the spirit of my life. I love you. But we shall never again speak of what passed between us."

Roan smashed his fist against the side of his chair. The pain forced him from his reverie.

"Saints be damned!" Leaning forward, he rested his elbows on his knees and kneaded his throbbing hand. More the fool he was. He cast glances in both directions to see if anyone had witnessed his foolishness.

In the distance, two figures approached. The tall one with the lithe gait was Falcon. The other, shorter, stouter, who walked with an almost cock-sure stride could be none other than Warren Quade.

Instantly, anger seized Roan. "Why does the man show himself now? Is it some sort of torture to taunt me with what he has and I want?"

As though a hand of peace descended onto his shoulder, he softened his words. "Why should I be angry with the man? He's done not one whit against me. She went back to him, to the Q-C of her own free will." With the words came the realization that he was truly glad to see his friend again.

"There he is, Mister Quade," Falcon said, gesturing toward Roan. "Almost as good as new." He turned to go, adding over his shoulder, "I'll see you in the morning, Roan."

"Would you kindly make it early, me friend?"

Falcon waved an acknowledgment and retreated, leaving Quade and Roan alone.

Roan rose to his feet and held out his hand in greeting. " 'Tis me friend, Warren Quade, and it's me that's happy to see you."

"Damn! You don't know how good it is to see you, old boy. I thought for a while I wouldn't again. You must have been drug through the coals while the fire still burned."

"Something like that."

"Tula said you were all right now." Quade's gaze traversed the length of Roan's body. "You don't look all right to me."

"Aye, I can understand your saying that. Me clothes hang a bit loose. But with a few more days I'll be good as new." Roan motioned toward the tipi. "Might we move inside, me friend? The evening air puts a bit of a chill in me bones and standing up to converse never was one of me better abilities."

"It is more relaxing to sit, isn't it?" Quade followed Roan inside where both of them seated themselves, facing each other, on the pallet.

"Tell me, Warren Quade, why does it take me good friend so long coming to see me?"

Warren's hand plucked nervously at the hair on the buffalo robe and studied the unconscious movement. "Lots of reasons, Roan, but I suppose the most important was your death."

"Saints be moved, me death?"

"Hell, yes. I figured you were dead the way Falcon described your condition and, from what Tula told me, he wasn't far wrong. My God, man, I could have understood had you been shot or if the whole damn Double S crew jumped you and beat the crap out of you. But a grizzly? Hell, no. I saw a man once after one of those sonsabitches finished with him. I was sick to my stomach two weeks after."

"Aye. It would have been the same with me had it not been for me friend, Patch."

"Patch?" Quade's eyebrows rose in question, then the answer came to him. "Oh, yes, the wolf. Tula said he saved your life. He must be one hell of an animal."

"It's that he is for certain. But getting back to your visit, Warren Quade. You surely must have heard that I didn't die."

Quade shook his head. "No, by God. Until Tula returned, nobody told me a damn thing. I figured after a while, when Tula hadn't come back, that you must be alive or that something had happened to her. I was about to come here to find out what was going on when that damned Azle Steppe rode in."

"Steppe again, was it? With still another offer for your land, no doubt."

"You're right. He said if I didn't sell, he'd get it his way. I'm telling you, Roan, the bastard's crazy dangerous."

"Aye. Dangerous as dynamite and just as explosive."

"I figured it best then to stay where I was. I had my men on guard day and night. When a week passed without anything happening, I was set to come here again, but Tula and your friend, Thax Hilton, showed up."

"He's a good man, Mister Hilton is. Did you hire him?"

"I did that. He's the reason I dared come to see you. But there's an even bigger reason I had to come, Roan. Tula."

Roan leaned forward, gripping Quade's arm. "She's not been hurt, has she?"

"Not the way you mean, Roan, but she's hurting all right — inside. Like I did when Josie died. Like you did when you lost Katie." Quade struggled to his feet and paced between the tipi entrance and back again. "The hell of it is, I think I'm in love with the woman after all this time."

"Think!" Roan thundered. "You *think* you're in love with her. How is it that you don't *know?*"

"I know this. I was in two kinds of hell while she was gone. I wanted to tell her when she returned, but she acted so damned different. I kept putting it off. She hasn't had anything to do with me, hardly talked to me. Then the night before I left to come here, I passed her room. She was crying, Roan — real tears. An Indian woman who seldom before showed her feelings and she was sobbing."

Roan couldn't speak past the lump in his throat.

Quade went on. "It got me thinking. The last few times after you visited the ranch, she remained distant for days. When Falcon told us you'd been hurt, she went crazy. Cried then, too. Wanted her horse saddled immediately. Couldn't wait to get here."

He resumed his pacing. Roan's eyes followed his nervous stride back and forth.

"I began thinking she might be in love with you, McCrae." He drew in a deep breath and exhaled slowly. "Is she?"

Roan couldn't answer. He stared at his hands clenched together in his lap. Quade sat down again, his words coming slowly, deliberately. "What happened here, Roan? She *is* in love with you. I know that now. Did she say so?"

Roan raised his head, looking straight into Quade's eyes. "Aye, Warren Quade, she spoke of love, but only when she thought I was drawing me last breath. Her Indian ways it was — asking me to take the words of her heart on me journey of death."

Quade nodded. "Sounds like Tula."

"And now she tells me we're never to speak of it again."

Both men sat for a long time without speaking, deep in their own thoughts. Roan broke the silence. "Would you be doing me a favor, Warren Quade?"

"Anything I can."

It took a few seconds for Roan to find the right words, wanting more than anything to protect

Tula. "You were telling me you believed you loved her."

"It's true, Roan."

"Then search your heart, man. Make certain. See to it Josie's ghost is at rest and be just as certain Tula's first above all, including your ranch. You talked to me straight once, Warren Quade, and it was me taking your advice. When you're sure in your own heart, me friend —" He paused, knowing he was about to plunge himself into eternal loneliness. His voice quavered as he continued, "Give me love, me Tula Moon, a good decent life. Ask her to be your wife."

Quade didn't answer for so long Roan thought he had forgotten the subject of their talk. Finally, he placed his hand on Roan's shoulder. "That's a damn decent thing for you to say, old friend, when both of us know how the land lies — she loves you and you love her."

The time seemed right for a lighter moment. Roan tried to make it so. "Faith, man, never have I tried to hide me feelings for the woman. But I have nothing to offer her. She's used to fine things and you can be giving them to her."

"Damn it, Roan. I know about those bastards burning your place. I'll help you build it back."

"Nay. Thanks the same. Should I go back now, I'd be for killing Jake Tanner and likely Azle Steppe as well — for something already done." He shook his head. "Nay. It's a pair of evil men they are. Someone will kill them one day, but I think it'll not be meself. Tomorrow, I'll be taking

Patch to the north to stay. I'll be staying also."

"North! Where? Why?"

Night crept over the land. The light in the tipi faded. Roan never noticed.

He answered, "It's me wish to settle in the Saskatchewan Territory. Some call it 'the far country.' For meself, it's a peaceful place where there be no guns, only quiet and" — he caught himself before he added "loneliness," finishing lamely — "no people. I'm called 'the wolfer,' a loner, you'll recall. I'll be that again."

Roan stoked the fire and settled back, saying no more. Quade was equally silent. When he did speak, the word came with such suddenness, such fierceness, it startled Roan. "Damn!" He rose to his feet.

Roan did the same.

"I have to leave, Roan. It's a long trip. And Tula waits. I'll do as you ask." He slipped his arm around Roan's shoulders. "You're like a brother, a brother I never had. I'll miss you."

"I'll be missing you as well, Warren Quade. You be like me own, too."

"So long," Quade said, and hurried through the entryway.

Roan settled beside the fire to warm his hands, which had grown cold with the thought of leaving forever. "So long," he whispered into the emptiness of the night. "Take care of me darling. She's me life."

Tears brimmed over onto his cheeks and fell onto his clasped hands.

Chapter Thirteen

The next morning Roan and Falcon stood outside the tipi. Roan's belongings, packed and ready, lay in a pile at their feet.

"Friend Falcon, would you be so kind as to fetch me dun and pack horse?" Roan asked. "While you're about it, I'll be loading these wee beasties into me trap."

Falcon nodded and walked away, heading for the grazing grounds. Roan went the opposite direction toward the glade. Patch and his mate usually were gone in the mornings when he worked. If the angel of luck rested on his shoulder, the two wolves would stay away at least until he got the pups inside the cage.

As he moved through the gloom of the glade, he caught a hint of movement to his left. He halted and peered through the trees into the thick undergrowth.

Nothing.

The hairs on his neck rose in warning. Again, he squinted into the darkness. A brief glimpse of something dark gray, close to the ground gave another suggestion of movement. Saints be damned. Every morning since he found their lair, both Patch and the bitch had been away, hunting. Early morning was the time for all animals to feed. Now when he really needed their absence, his luck failed.

He waited and watched a few minutes longer,

but there was nothing more. Maybe they were heading away from him. He moved on through the glade and out into the bright lea.

Still apprehensive, he headed for the trap. The snap of a twig whirled him around a third time. Instinctively, he crouched low to the ground. The figure of a man wound through the brush. Smoke spewed from the barrel of a rifle a second before the sharp report.

Heat from the bullet singed his shirt collar.

He vaulted for cover. Another bullet split the air, brushing close to his face. He touched his cheekbone to assure himself there was no blood.

Crabbing his way toward a clump of wild berry bushes, he uttered silent pleas to his saints as slug after slug whacked tree trunks near his head.

A fallen pine blocked the pathway. He dove behind it and lay still. Between labored breaths, he listened for footsteps. Who the hell? Tanner? No doubt. Tanner — or Steppe, maybe both.

He slowed his breathing. He risked lifting his head enough to peer around the end of the log. A slug plowed the ground, spraying powdery earth into his face. He jerked back, half blinded by the dust in his eyes. A low guttural laugh grated in his ears, followed by the graveled voice. "You're dead, Irish. You're dead, you understand me? And that damn wolf is next."

"Come ahead, Jake Tanner. You'll not be finding it as easy as you think, you murdering rakesail."

Easy? Faith, Tanner would never find it more

so. Roan had no protection. His rifle remained in the lodge with the rest of his pack. Leaves crunched underfoot, louder, more distinct with each step.

Tanner's rifle exploded again. Splinters flew. Roan crowded close to the dead tree, pressed his body against the ground as though he wanted to become part of it.

A wild, piercing scream reverberated through the glade, followed by three shots in close succession. Tanner swore. Immediately after, someone ran. Roan peered over the log. Falcon ran into the clearing, hefted Roan's rifle to his shoulder and loosed three more shots.

Seconds later, horse's hooves pounded away.

Exhausted, Roan seated himself on the log and shook his head. In scant seconds, Falcon stood over him. Roan glanced up at his friend. "I see you found me rifle."

Falcon nodded. "I remembered seeing it in your pack. I was almost to the horses when I heard the first shot, so I grabbed the gun on my way back. Sorry that bushwhacking bastard got away. You all right?"

"Aye, aside from having the bejesus scared from me. Right before you showed up, I think I may have shit me pants."

Falcon roared with laughter so contagious Roan couldn't help joining him. "If that's true, Roan, would you mind walking downwind of me?"

Roan gave him a playful nudge in the ribs and

moved back a couple of paces. Falcon grabbed him and pulled him closer.

"Well, me friend," Roan said as the two headed for camp, "there'll be no trap set for Patch's lady today. The commotion'll be bringing her back to check on her bairn."

Tomorrow would be soon enough, but it had to be tomorrow.

"Quit your yipping, scamp," he scolded the wriggling bundle of fur in his hand. "Your den mate'll think I'm throttling you and they'll not be so easy to catch. Stop it now, you scalawag. Me finger ain't your morning meal."

Just as Roan placed the last pup inside the enclosure, the first two decided to seek their freedom. Roan snatched them and thrust them in with the others. He glanced around. Nervous sweat rolled down his face. "Now you lookee here, you wee whelps, you can't keep escaping me trap. Your Ma catches me here, it's more than me fingers she'll be chewing. Get in there and stay put. You'll understand one day it was your lives I was saving."

With sturdy twigs from a nearby tree, he wove a partition that succeeded in keeping the pups inside. He breathed in relief then hurried to the edge of the trees where he could safely watch for the wolves' return.

Falcon appeared beside him. "I see you got it finished."

Roan nodded. "Where did you tie the horses?"

164

"At the edge of the woods. Listen, friend Roan, have you given any thought to what you'll do when you get to the north? Or wherever you plan to wander?"

"I'll do what you're so fond of doing — hunt, fish, and lie in the sun."

"Sounds good. I know of a cabin in the north territory. If you like, you could stay there and the braves and I could visit occasionally."

"A cabin you say. And whose would it be?"

"My father knew an old mountain man who lived there. It was built a good forty years ago, but it'll keep the wind from whistling up the tail of your shirt."

Talking with Falcon this way calmed Roan. Nearly forgotten was the episode with Tanner and his apprehension as he loaded the bitch's pups. He was hardly aware that nearly half an hour had passed.

"I'm telling you, Roan, you can catch fish in the streams up there that are as big as —"

Roan laid a silencing hand on Falcon's arm. "Sh-h-h. There they be. When she goes inside, I'll make a run for the trap door and tie it shut. You be bringing the horses."

Patch was the first to sense something wrong. With Shadow close behind, he ran toward the cage. After a brief sniff at one of the pups inside the partition, he turned and left the trap, standing close beside it, his head twisting first one way, then the other, as though he searched for an explanation to the plight of his young ones.

The bitch growled low while she darted around the cage. When she located the entrance, she ran inside, clawing and biting furiously at the sticks that kept her children separated from her.

Roan smiled, broke cover and dashed for the opening. He had scarcely reached the trap door before she spied him and snarled, baring sharp fangs, snapping threats at this intruding human who had disturbed her family. With nimble fingers, Roan secured the door only seconds before Shadow tore down the partition and gathered her young. Like burrowing moles, they wriggled beneath her and suckled.

Using a lariat for a harness on the big work horse Falcon delivered, Roan fastened the travois poles securely. "Would you kindly tell me more about this cabin?" he asked. "There'd be no one living there now?"

"The old man passed into the spirit world several seasons past," Falcon answered.

"Then perhaps you'd be good enough to draw a map or give me some sort of directions." Roan checked the bindings around the cage. Patch remained close to his mate, who had calmed some and was now fondling her young, licking their fur into tiny whorls. Each time Roan passed near, she snarled and snapped.

"Certainly I could draw you a map," Falcon said. "It would probably get you there."

"Probably, is it? And how would I not get there?"

"I was going to say I would rather lead you."

Roan paused in his labor. "You would do that, friend Falcon?"

"If you wouldn't mind my company."

"I would like nothing better."

"Done then." Falcon smiled, creasing the scar on his cheek until it nearly closed his eye. He pointed through the trees. "Go straight ahead. You will find a trail. I'll catch up as soon as I get my horse and supplies."

The muscular young Indian retreated toward the camp. In Roan's mind echoed the words Tula had spoken of Falcon. "He was born a few years too late. Reservation life is too tame for the likes of Falcon."

It was a fact, plain and simple. Roan climbed into the dun's saddle and drew in deep draughts of fresh air. How wonderful to be well again, well enough to climb aboard his mount. All that marred his pleasure was uncertainty about the life that lay ahead of him. But treading new ground was better than lying around feeling sorry about the way things were.

He pulled the pack horse's lead rope, kicked the dun into a fast walk.

He found the trail and rode a short way into the open country before Falcon, leading a pack horse loaded with supplies, joined him. Falcon handed him a large parcel and laughed. "It's meat and cakes from the women. They say Tac-se-nas is too skinny. They would rather have a fat brother."

Why didn't people think the Indians had humor? Good people, they were. "By the saints, I'll be missing them, Falcon. I'm wondering if I'll ever see them again."

"I would say the answer to that would be up to you and the Father Spirit, Roan. My people will always welcome you. Be assured of that. I think you should know, too, that the place I am taking you is lonely and wild. I'm told a man who lives alone in such a wilderness can go mad."

"Aye, loneliness. It's something I know about."

Because of the travois, their pace was slow. Roan didn't mind. He was in no hurry. The further he and Falcon traveled, the wilder, more rugged the terrain became. Lush green valleys stippled with trees yielded to swift streams, deep lakes as clear as the mountain air. Trails wound around craggy mountains, their peaks looming high above.

On the first day, the second, too, Roan felt exhausted before the day ended. They made camp early. Each successive day, his strength built.

The land was beautiful, even when it became treacherous with rock slides and raging rivers. In its fury was a splendor Roan loved.

On the eighth day of travel, the two came off a long hogback ridge that sloped downward to meet the shore of a large sky-blue lake. "We are here," Falcon said. "Right around the lake is the cabin."

"The sight takes me breath away," Roan commented. "The water's so clear and I'm thinking deep also."

"My friends and I have swum the lake many times. We call it *Lanai Ka-ti-wa*. It means deep moon. At night, when the moon comes up, you believe it rises right out of the lake bed. The water is warm on top, but a few feet down it turns icy cold. The brothers believe Lunai goes through the center of the earth and surfaces again on the other side."

Roan followed as Falcon led the way around the lakeshore. "There," Falcon said suddenly, pointing ahead. "Not beautiful, I suppose, but you'll never find a home as solid. The old man built it well."

Straight, peeled logs formed the walls of the structure half hidden among the trees. A far cry from the cottage he had built for Katie, but serviceable and sturdy. He could make it his own. "It's a place I can call me home," Roan commented.

"You'll want to turn the she-wolf loose first, I suppose," Falcon said.

"Aye. She's been a prisoner in that cage days too long."

They secured Falcon's pack horse to a hitching post and rode on for another hundred yards or so behind the cabin. Roan eased the travois down and cut the cage door's binding. Quickly, he retreated.

The snarling bitch wolf hit the opening with a

169

powerful lunge and kept running. Within seconds, she was out of sight. Gently, Roan lifted the pups to safety and, using a hefty club — "Me *shillelagh*," he told Falcon — he destroyed the cage.

Patch stood nearby watching Roan's every move. As pieces of the trap fell to the ground, he turned, ears pointing toward the trees into which his mate had disappeared.

"This be your home now, Patch me friend. Go tell her she'll be safe here. Bring her back to her bairn."

Patch hesitated.

"Go, boy." Roan snapped his fingers and pointed.

Patch darted toward the woods. Roan could hear him howling for the she-wolf, the sound diminishing as the big wolf searched deeper into the forest. Then, silence.

"I reckon they'll be coming back soon," Roan said. "I'll be building a fire and making some coffee."

"I prefer tea," Falcon said.

"Then tea it will be."

The two men walked back to the cabin, unloaded bedrolls and food. "I'll stake out the animals, friend Roan. You build that fire and make the coffee."

"Tea," Roan corrected, slapping Falcon on the shoulder as they laughed.

"We have two pans. Make both."

Roan surveyed the place that would be his

home — how long he didn't know. A table and two long benches hewn from rough cedar logs were the only furnishings. A long stone fireplace, a small window next to the front door occupied one entire wall. Six bunk beds, also made of logs and covered with grass mats, decked two more walls. The fourth was bare except for the back door and a small log shelf used to hold flour, sugar and such other provisions as might absorb dampness from the dirt floor.

Using logs from a crude kindling bin near the hearth, Roan built a roaring fire and set two pans of water to boil on flat rocks. The aroma of strong coffee and rich tea brought a smile to Falcon's face when he came in.

Dark moved over the land while the two sat sipping tea and coffee and eating gos-kema with honey. Falcon nodded toward the bunks. "My brothers and I built those when bad weather chased us inside."

"They'll be coming in handy when you visit me again," Roan returned. They were friends and friends would be looking in on him from time to time.

Falcon yawned, tossed his bedroll on one of the bunks and stretched out on it. Within minutes, he was asleep.

"I guess I'll be checking on me young charges before I join you, friend Falcon," Roan said to the prone figure. Slipping through the back door, he edged his way toward where he had released the pups.

They were gone.

Roan smiled, staring into the darkness. Crickets and tree frogs chirped in cadence. Nearby, an owl hooted. In the distance, the mournful howl of a wolf sang to him, answered by a second howl, much closer. Patch appeared through the trees and trotted to Roan's side, nuzzling his hand.

Roan squatted and wrapped an arm around the big wolf's neck. "This be your home now, boy. There'll be no guns here. No Jake Tanner nor the others like him to hunt you down. You and your family are safe here." He rubbed the bristly fur along Patch's nose. "You be seeing to your mate now. See her as much as you can."

As though he understood, Patch turned and disappeared into the trees.

Chapter Fourteen

Contentment remained over the next days as Falcon and Roan swam in the lake and relaxed over what was left of the good food prepared by the Sioux women. Roan relished the warmth of the surface water, avoided the icy depths.

Falcon, on the other hand, dove deep and surfaced with his teeth chattering.

The mineral water loosened the scabs on Roan's wounds. They peeled off, leaving healthy pink scars. The healing was complete. He stretched out on the lakeshore and absorbed the sun's energy each day.

"Come on," Falcon urged Roan. "I know a stream a short way from here where you can pull trout to the bank as fast as you can dip your line."

He hadn't lied. Later that evening, their bellies were full from fish fried in one of the blackened skillets they had brought.

Late one morning, Roan and Falcon followed a small stream that meandered through a long narrow valley. Their attention riveted on the ground, they searched for game tracks. It was a game. Each tried to identify the species of animal that had left the track.

When they came upon the huge padded prints with long claw lines, both men chanted as one, "Grizzly."

A roar no more than thirty feet from them cut

their word in mid-breath. The grizzly rose on his hind legs and thundered a second warning.

Falcon wheeled his mount. "He's going to charge, Roan. Let's go!"

Roan's dun was willing to follow Falcon, but Roan wasn't. Instead of fear, he felt anger. He held the dun in check long enough to jerk his rifle from the boot and dismount. The horse broke loose from his grasp and fled.

The bear, with its deceptively slow-looking gait, charged straight at Roan.

Roan cocked his rifle and fired. The bullet dug a ridge in the dirt a few feet in front of the oncoming grizzly. He lunged forward.

Roan darted to the right and aimed the rifle. The slug plowed along the bear's hind quarter. In mid-stride, the animal turned, ready to fight the thing that had attacked from the rear.

With the bear's backside toward him again, Roan fired another shot, parting the hair on the other side.

The grizzly jerked around in that direction. Twice more Roan fired. He twisted back and forth searching for his attacker.

"You be wanting to keep part of that fat rump of yours, you'd best be for running, old bugger."

One more sting and the bear took his advice, stubby legs carrying it up the gentle slope of the valley. Roan sent two more shots in the general direction.

The bear sped its pace, turned sideways, its wounded rear trying to outrun its front.

Roan laughed. "I didn't think you were moving at your top speed, old boy."

He searched for Falcon. Suddenly, he choked back the mirth and ran toward the Indian, sprawled on his hands and knees shaking with some sort of spasms.

"Friend Falcon, what would be ailing you?"

As he neared, he sighed with relief. His Indian friend wasn't caught in the throes of convulsions, unless laughter could be so considered.

"Damn you, Roan McCrae," Falcon choked out, tears streaming down his face. "Damn you anyway."

"Damn me for what?"

"I laughed so hard I fell off my horse." Falcon struggled to his feet, wiped his face and leaned across his horse's broad back. "I never in my life saw anything like that. When I turned around and saw you standing there facing that charging bear, I thought I had a crazy white-eyed brother. Why didn't you run?"

Roan shook his head. "It's a tad stupid I was, I'll admit, but the beast made me mad. Two of the devils I've seen of late and both were charging me. I wanted to teach this one a lesson."

"Well, I would say you accomplished that. When I saw you raise your rifle, I thought you were going to kill the brute. I wouldn't have blamed you."

Roan's brows arched in question. "And why now should I be killing a fine animal like that? King of the woods, he is. It's his nature to attack those he thinks are threatening his domain. Sure, it was you, Falcon, you told me that."

"True," Falcon answered, "but not all wakandas are good. The spirit of the grizzly is angry, mean."

"Are you saying I should have killed the beast then?"

"I would have, if I'd had the nerve." Falcon looked off down the valley. Roan's dun grazed nearly a mile away. The brave leaped astraddle of his mount and held out his hand. "Come on, let's go stop that horse of yours before he runs off a cliff." He pulled Roan up behind him and kicked the big paint into a run. With a grin, he said over his shoulder, "I'm a lot like that dun of yours, Roan."

"And how is that?"

"I have horse sense."

Roan punched the Indian in the ribs. "Would you be saying I don't?"

Falcon grunted. "If you did have, friend, I wouldn't have seen what I just saw. That bear went crazy trying to catch whatever kept biting him on the ass." He slapped his leg and roared with laughter.

Roan joined him, enjoying the release of tension the laughter afforded.

They lay on the shoreline absorbing the afternoon sun. Roan sat up, suddenly. "Do you see, friend Falcon, we're about to have some company?"

Falcon turned his attention to the direction Roan indicated.

Riders galloped over the mountain ridge and down the steep incline.

Caution urged Roan and Falcon to the protection of the cabin and the closeness of their guns. They watched from the doorway as the riders moved around the lake, coming constantly closer.

"Hec-ta!" Falcon shouted. "It's Gray Fox and some of the brothers."

Roan, aware for the first time he had held his breath, released it and drank in gulps of air. "Aye, and it's glad I am to see them. But look how their horses are lathered. Why did they run them so?"

"Something is wrong. I planned to return to the reservation tomorrow. It looks like I may leave sooner."

The braves skidded their mounts to a halt. Gray Fox leaped from his horse and spoke in the Sioux tongue, his words tumbling over each other.

Falcon held up his hand to silence the stout-framed Indian. He turned to Roan. "Fox says the Double S raided the Q-C. Killed some of the crew and took it over."

Roan moved closer. "Is Tula all right?"

With the initial impact of his news delivered, Gray Fox relaxed and spoke in broken English.

"Tula okay. Send white eye to reservation. Say Warren Quade hurt. Tula, black brother take him to shaman."

"Warren's hurt? They'll be on the reservation then?" Roan asked.

Fox shook his head. "Town closer. Tula take Quade to shaman in Buckhorn town."

"How bad is he hurt?" Falcon asked.

Gray Fox shrugged. "The white eye say hurt bad. No more. We stay now or go?"

"We go," Roan said without hesitation. He looked to Falcon for confirmation. "Warren Quade be me friend. It's us who should be helping him."

A wide smile winked the Indian's scarred eye. "We're with you, Roan, but going into Buckhorn? I don't know. A good many of the white eyes there are not too fond of us."

"Town ain't where you'll be needed. Taking the ranch back is."

"Hai-ek!" Falcon shouted. "We go! Now!"

"Aye, we go," Roan replied. "As soon as I find Patch and let him know I'll be coming back."

Trail weary and covered with grime, Roan reined down the main street of Buckhorn. There would be time later for a bath and an hour or two of sleep. Now, his thoughts were with Warren Quade and how badly Quade might be injured.

Shame burned his face when he found Quade's predicament shoved aside by the vision of Roan holding Tula Moon in his arms.

At the hotel, Room 12, Roan rapped softly on the door.

"Come in," called a muffled voice.

Roan entered to find himself staring down the barrel of a .45 gripped in the hand of Warren Quade. "What the hell?" Quade's eyes widened. "Roan McCrae! I sure wasn't expecting you."

"It's me hope you weren't since you greeted me with that wee piece of hardware."

Warren shoved the gun beneath his pillow and eased himself against the headboard. "Maybe I should use it," he said. "I thought you intended to stay in the north country."

"And well I did." Roan seated himself on a nearby chair. "But I was told you'd had some trouble here."

"Sure you weren't told I was in a bad way — dying maybe."

"Aye, I was told you weren't the best."

"So you thought you'd come and claim Tula."

Roan frowned. Something in Quade's voice wasn't teasing. "I came because —"

"You don't need to explain. She's down the hall."

"I'll be seeing her directly. First I wanted to make certain you were fit." The frown still creased his brow. He studied Quade's face and found little of the brotherhood he'd shared with the man these past years. "You think I'm here because —"

"We both know why you're here. I should never have believed the two of you. I should have known there was more than just caring for wounds there on the reservation."

"It was there you told me you understood, Warren Quade. And there, you told me you loved Tula Moon and intended to marry her. Did you do that — did you marry the girl?"

"Not that it's any of your business. No, I didn't."

"And why not?"

"How could I marry her? She won't let me near her. Whatever you two did when you were together on the reservation ruined any chance I might have had."

"You're wrong, Warren Quade." Roan's anger rose. He tried to stifle it. "There was nothing between meself and Tula Moon except words. It was the way she wanted, her believing the way she does about devotion and the ancient spirits of her people. She made me give me word that there'd be no mention of it again. If she won't consent to be your wife, her decision's none of me own doing."

"It's damn sure not my doing. I've tried everything to make her see how much I care. She never smiles. The warmth is gone from her eyes. Oh, she waits on me, cooks for me, keeps the house, but aside from that, the only time I see a light in her eyes is when your name is mentioned."

"I came here as a friend, Warren Quade, to help you save your ranch. If it's an enemy you want me to be, you'd best think twice. I'm a man who doesn't like to lose."

"Is that a threat?"

"Nay, it's me promise. I'll do the job I came to do because I've given me word to Falcon and the brothers. But I'll not leave here without Tula Moon, if she'll be having me. You disappoint me and me thinking you were a different sort of man."

"I swear to you, Roan, you take Tula with you when you go and it'll be over my dead body."

"Perhaps that can be arranged, Mister Quade. I came to visit me friend, me brother who'd been hurt. I'll take me departure now from a man I find I don't really know."

Roan got up. At the doorway, he turned and pointed his finger straight at Quade. "You'd be wise to do some thinking about your words today. In Ireland, a man is poor indeed without true friends, no matter how wealthy he be. You'll die in poverty if you don't change your ways. You're a damn fool for not trusting those who've given you nothing but their loyalty."

As he stepped into the hallway, Quade called to him.

He didn't answer. Instead, he strode to Tula's quarters and knocked. When she opened the door, stood there before him, he couldn't speak. He could only drink in her beauty and her sorrow. The long black hair, usually worn in two braids which cascaded over her shoulders, now hung in a single limp plait down the center of her back. Dark half circles beneath her eyes declared the lack of sleep she had suffered. Her face was pale and drawn, her usually rosy lips pallid, pressed into a firm line.

He ached to hold her, yearned to smell the clean scent of her hair, to feel her body warm and supple against his.

She took a hesitant step toward him. It was enough. He closed the distance and reached for her.

She moved back into the room. "No," she said softly. "You promised."

He could hear the longing in her voice. "I love you, Tula me girl."

"By all I hold sacred, Roan McCrae, I wish it could be different."

"It's your heart you have to listen to, not the ways of your people. Neither your God or mine meant for us to be apart. Whatever keeps us that way is wrong. I've just been with Warren Quade. He tells me you'll have nothing to do with him. It's one of us or the other, Tula me love. You're not being true even to your own beliefs this way." He turned to go.

"Roan?"

"I came here to do a job, to save the Q-C. I'll be back for me answer from you a little later."

"The answer won't be any different then, Roan. I made my promise to Wakan Tanka."

"Aye, and you made me vow as well, but it's one vow I intend to be breaking."

"No. Roan, you must respect —"

"It's wrong. It's me word I should never have given and I'm taking it back this second."

He started down the stairs, nearly colliding

with Thax Hilton. "I saw you come in," Hilton said. "I'm surely glad you're here. I've just been talking with the marshal. You and I need to discuss some things."

Roan chanced one last glance at Tula. She stood on the second floor landing, her eyes filled with tears.

Once outside, he swallowed back the lump of despair that threatened to spill over. For a moment, he wondered when his memory of his dear Katie became so distant. He could scarcely recall when he hadn't loved Tula. He shook his head to clear his mind and turned to Hilton. "Now, Mister Hilton, what is it you've learned?"

"Several things, Roan. One of which is that we can't count on Marshal Tindal for anything. He's jumping at his own shadow since the Double S crew rode into town. Word's gotten around that they stole Quade's ranch."

"Were you there, me friend? Were you at the Q-C when they come?"

Hilton nodded. "Most of Quade's crew scattered like jackrabbits running from the hounds. Three — only three — stayed behind and helped us fight. Steppe's men shot them down."

" 'Tis a wonder they didn't kill Warren Quade and Tula as well."

"Hell, Roan, they knew they'd owe the devil if they shot a woman, especially an Indian woman. They'd have the whole reservation on their tails."

"Aye, it's that they have anyway."

Hilton raised his eyebrows. "What do you mean?"

"We stopped at the ranch before I come to see me friend Quade."

"And?"

"We watched the place for a couple of hours. There are at least twenty men."

"I'd guessed as much. Steppe had a small army with him when they attacked the ranch."

"But we'll have more. Falcon will have at least thirty waiting for us there tomorrow night."

Hilton grinned. "The tide turns."

"Aye, and Azle Steppe will be caught in it. At least that's me hope." He hesitated a moment, then asked, "But you said Steppe and his bunch of scurvy lice had come to town?"

"Half a dozen of them are at the Last Chance. I saw their horses tied out front. That was why I went to talk to Tindal. Like I said, he'll give us no help. Whatever we do, we'll be doing it on our own."

"Well then, we'll do what we have to do."

"There's something more, Roan."

"And that is?"

"Steppe's hired Bino Smith. Do you know who he is?"

"That I do — by reputation. Once, I was in a pub — er — a saloon in Scarsdale and two fellas was talking about this Bino Smith. A man fast with a gun, they said. A man with hair and eyes like the albino stallions the rangemen find so valuable."

"That's where he got his name — Bino. Albino people are rare, Roan, but they exist. He's a strange-looking one, although I've seen him only once and then just a glance."

"And is he fast? As fast as you?"

"Some say so. Something I learned early on, Roan, is there's always someone faster or more accurate. You have to be smart, too. I've heard Bino Smith is all three, but he's easy to anger and that's on our side. An angry man doesn't think straight."

"What else do you know of this Smith?"

"He gives my profession a bad name."

"How so?"

"He likes to kill, not just for money or fame. He kills for pleasure — toys with his victims, tortures them. Any man who's about to die has a right to do so quickly."

"And that's how you handle such, Mister Hilton? Quick?"

"I have to have a good reason to kill someone, Roan. I have to know the person deserves to die. You should know that. I was hired to kill you."

"There's some think I deserve it, too." Warren Quade's face edged itself into his memory and he felt a surge of sadness. "But we were talking about this Mister Smith and he's on the side of Azle Steppe, is he? 'Tis fine, 'tis fine. Our side has your speed with a gun and Falcon's cunning. What more do we need?"

"What we need is the sheriff and his deputies. We need the law. Even Tindal is better than no

185

law. You and I, if we go looking for trouble with Steppe and his men, have absolutely no authority."

"Me Da always said a man is the law if he has right on his side. Do you not find that true, Thax Hilton?"

"True enough, but it wouldn't impress a court. Gunmen sometimes think twice before they tangle with someone wearing a badge." Hilton nodded toward the marshal's office. "Let's pay another call on Mister Tindal, shall we? Maybe the two of us can persuade him to help in some way."

"You look like a man with an idea."

"A small one." Hilton grinned. "It may not work, but it's worth a try. Unless you have a better one."

"Nay, when me old friend Warren Quade spurned me hand of friendship, all me ideas took wing." Again, the sadness washed over his soul, chilling him.

"Quade did what?"

"It's a misunderstanding, we'll say for now." He clenched his fist. "Let's be for seeing the marshal. Maybe we can make the cowardly cur understand the need."

He wanted to purge the argument between him and Quade, but it hung like a shroud. Warren Quade had convinced him to stop spending his days brawling in some pub. Possibly, Quade had saved his life that day.

Quade was a true friend and now, Tula Moon

had come between them. How did a man choose between friendship and love? When he was a child, Da always told him real friendship was a golden treasure that never tarnished. It should be held close to the heart, protected and nurtured.

Quade's words had hurt though. More than that was the agony he suffered from Tula's stubborn beliefs.

Chapter Fifteen

Marshal Vern Tindal hadn't changed in appearance since the last time Roan spent a night in jail. The Marshal wore striped pants, a white shirt and a string tie that drooped over his sunken chest.

He gave every appearance of being at ease when Roan and Hilton entered the simple log structure that housed the marshal's office and the jail. His feet, in highly polished boots, rested atop the desk. His hat, tipped forward, shaded his eyes. His hands were folded across his bulging paunch. He had removed his gunbelt and tossed it to the side of the desk farthest from him.

When they entered, his feet thudded to the floor, the boots making a simultaneous "thunk." He leaned forward, his hand searching for his gun butt. His eyes, still heavy with sleep, focused slowly.

"McCrae, Hilton," he said. "What the hell do you want?" He shook his head and resumed his original position, chair tilted, feet propped.

Roan moved closer, edging behind the desk, near the marshal's chair. "Mister Hilton and me would appreciate it, Marshal Tindal, if you'd give us a wee hand bringing Azle Steppe and his crew into your jail."

"I'm busy." Tindal settled his hat a little lower on his face.

"I can see that," Roan retorted. He shot his right foot forward, catching the front leg of the chair. A quick yank and the chair crashed to the wood floor.

Tindal flailed his arms trying to catch himself in midfall. His head bumped against the wall with a resounding crack.

"You Irish sonofabitch!" he shouted, picking himself up and rubbing the back of his head.

"I'd consider it a matter of honor," Roan said, "if you'd refrain from calling me names. You see, I'm willing to overlook any you might have called meself up to now just so long as you come along nicely with Mister Hilton and me to the saloon."

"I can't do that."

"Can't, Marshal?" Hilton asked, his eyes narrowed. "Or won't?"

"It's all right, friend Hilton," Roan soothed. "The marshal here can't help wearing the white feather. Coward that he is, I think we may have to convince him to do what's right."

"Convince me? I'm the law here, not you. If there's any convincing to be done —"

"But, you see, Marshal Tindal, Hilton and meself have a bit of a problem. The Double S men took something from a friend of ours and we're wanting them to return it. Can you understand that?"

Tindal pulled himself upright, still rubbing the spot on the back of his head. "Just get out of here, the both of you. The Q-C ranch is out of my jurisdiction."

"But the men that stole the Q-C and killed three men ain't," Roan returned. "Are you sure,

Marshal, you don't want to come along and do your duty?"

"It's none of my business."

"Aye. Well, me and Mister Hilton can handle it, I suppose, but we'll be needing you to swear us in as deputies. Facing Azle Steppe and his band of *barley swiggers* without benefit of badges would do us no good. You understand that, don't you?"

"I'll deputize the two of you," Tindal said with a derisive laugh. "When hell freezes over."

"That better be in the next two seconds," Hilton warned.

Tindal's attention shifted nervously to the black man. "I ain't afraid of you." The tremor in his voice turned his words to lies.

Roan pointed his finger in the marshal's face. "If you're not afraid of Mister Hilton, why is it you fear that murdering bunch of rakesails from the Double S?"

"I don't," Tindal shouted. "I told you, the Q-C is out of my jurisdiction. That's the sheriff's job —" His face beaded with sweat. Droplets rolled down his cheeks and dripped from his chin and jaw. His gaze wandered from Roan to Hilton and back again. He edged toward the desk, his hand slinking toward his gun. When he made his final move, he was slow.

Just as his fingertips touched the gun butt, Roan reached out, grasping the marshal's shirt. He jerked the lawman across the desk, Tindal's paunch landing hard on the wood top. A whoosh

190

escaped from Tindal's fat lips.

He yanked free and slid to his feet to keep the desk between him and Roan. "You drunken mick wolfer —"

Roan picked up the gun which had fallen to the floor and shoved it in his belt. Hilton righted the chair, grinning. Roan lifted Tindal and thrust him back into the seat.

He moved around to stand in front of the quaking marshal who blubbered, "No. No. He'll kill me. I tell you. He'll kill me." He repeated the phrase again and again, eyes wild with terror.

Roan looked at Hilton and shrugged.

Hilton strode forward and grasped Tindal's hair, lifting his head. With a swift motion, he backhanded the fat jowls. Spittle flew from the puffed lips. Hilton followed with a hard slap on the other side of Tindal's face.

"Straighten up," he told the lawman. "Straighten up or I'll kill you myself, you worthless slob."

Whimpering like a wounded pup, Tindal cowered.

"Bino Smith's over there, Hilton," he moaned. "If I go inside that saloon, he'll kill me sure. He as much as told me so."

"Then don't go. You'd be useless anyway. But you're going to deputize us. Badges and all."

Tindal sank back, nodding his head vigorously. "The badges are in that top drawer there."

Hilton retrieved two tin stars and handed one to Roan. As they pinned them on, Hilton said,

"Now, Tindal, swear us in."

"Raise your right hands. Swear to uphold the laws of Buckhorn."

"We swear," Roan and Hilton chimed in unison.

"Now, get out of here and leave me be," Tindal said.

"We'll do that, Marshal," Roan agreed. "But whilst we're about your business, you get yourself to the nearest telegraph and send for the sheriff and as many deputies as he can bring."

Tindal's eyes widened. "The nearest telegraph is in Scarsdale. Them Double S fellers see me leaving town, they'll shoot me for sure. Bino Smith done told me what I had to do to stay healthy."

Hilton interrupted. "Smith will be far too busy with me to notice what the hell you're doing." He looked up at the wall clock. "Twenty-eight hours from now — seven tomorrow evening — is plenty of time for the sheriff to get here. If he isn't you'll answer to me." He turned to Roan. "Ready?"

"Ready," Roan answered. They strode toward the door.

Over his shoulder, Hilton said, "Tindal, if that sheriff isn't here tomorrow evening, you better find a deep hole."

Roan crossed the street to where his horse was tied and lifted his rifle from the boot. As he and Hilton moved toward the saloon, he checked the load in his gun. "Would you be telling me how best we do this, Thax Hilton? Do we both go through the front door together, or — ?"

"Did anyone see you when you rode into town?"

"I'd not be knowing that for sure, but I think not."

Hilton nodded. "Might be we could surprise them then. You come through the back. Wait until you hear me speak before you let them know you're there."

"Give me a couple minutes before you go in," Roan said, and darted between two buildings to the alley behind the saloon.

Once he located the back door, he opened it quietly and stepped inside. A hallway led to the barroom. The only light came from a single dim lamp close to where he now stood.

Roan slid the bolt in place to lock the door in case one of the bar patrons was in the outhouse. No need risking some damn varmint slipping in on his backside after the drums started rolling.

He inched forward. Hilton thundered from inside the bar, "Anyone in here doesn't work for the Double S, it'd be wise if he left. Now!"

Boots stomped across the sawdusted floor. The swinging doors in the front opened and flapped several times as they closed.

Roan mentally pictured the barroom. The bar would be to his left as he entered, the front to the right. Hilton would be in that vicinity.

Roan stood where Hilton could see him. Hilton

nodded. Roan was in the right place. He clung to the hallway shadows.

Low, menacing, Hilton said, "Azle Steppe, you and these cutthroats of yours are under arrest for murder."

Steppe's high-pitched laugh grated. "From a killer to a playacting deputy marshal. Hilton, you're not serious."

"You'll soon find out how serious I am. All of you, unbuckle your gunbelts with one hand. Put the other hand on your heads. Do it careful, do it quick."

One of Steppe's men said in a mocking tone. "How you going to enforce that order, Hilton? There's six of us. Your gun ain't even drawed and I'm faster than you all by myself."

Roan's attention was drawn to Ben Shay, the bartender whose hand slowly moved beneath the bar. Roan stepped forward, cocking his rifle. The click echoed in the confines of the hallway. Shay's hand jerked back.

"Hilton's gun might not be at the ready, but it's certain this one is." Roan leveled a kick at the barkeep's flabby butt. "Get yourself out front, mister, and collect those guns."

Shay scurried around the bar with Roan behind him, sending another kick his way each time he slowed. Meanwhile Roan surveyed the others he and Hilton had to face.

Three of the men stood at the bar. Two others flanked Steppe at a table. One of them, young, mid-twenties, was easy to recognize. His long

194

white hair and pale eyes set in a pallid face labeled him as Bino Smith. He carefully removed his gunbelt with its cutaway holster.

The bartender's hand trembled as he reached for the gunfighter's weapon. The gun told a lot about Bino. It had no trigger or trigger guard. He was one who fanned the hammer. Fine if you were fast enough, but Roan wouldn't bet money on that style against a man who was fast with his trigger finger.

He edged closer to Hilton, all the while sizing up the tall slim cowboy who stood on the other side of Azle Steppe. He had seen him before — with Tanner. The men called him Lank. It fit him well, his belt cinched around a too-thin waist, gathering his dungarees so they fit.

Roan motioned to the three men at the bar. "Move over by your boss."

They complied.

Roan glared at the bartender. "Now, Ben, get the rest of those guns collected."

Ben picked up three more of the heavy weapons, laid them on the bar and went back after the others. He returned to Steppe and held out his hand.

"I don't carry a gun," Steppe said. "You stupid jackass, you know that."

Hilton laughed. "He doesn't have to, Ben. Not when he can afford to hire men like Bino there."

"Yeah, Hilton," Bino retorted. "Looks like I'll be earning my wages before this is over."

"I have a feeling you might at that."

Ben shuffled over to Lank, motioning toward the gunbelt.

Lank shook his head. "I believe I'll earn my wages now," he said. His prominent Adam's apple jumped up and down when he spoke. "I ain't wasting away in no damn jail." His hand darted to his side.

Hilton reached, but before his gun cleared leather, Roan's rifle exploded.

The bullet slammed into Lank's arm, spinning him halfway around. He screamed and crumpled into a chair. Eyes wide, he watched blood flow down his arm and drip from his fingertips onto the floor. He groaned. "My arm." He glared toward Roan. "You sonofabitch, you ruined my gun arm. I might as well be dead."

"You would be," Hilton said, "had it been my bullet."

"It was a stupid play, Lank," Bino remarked. "I'm faster than Hilton and I know it, but I ain't faster than a man with a cocked rifle."

Hilton's voice was low and angry. "That's twice you've said you're faster than me. Maybe it's time you proved it." The jet eyes flashed in fury. His thin lips were drawn tight. Bino's words had roused the killer blood in Thaxter Hilton again.

He pointed toward Lank. "Ben, get his gun. Lay it on the bar. And . . . give Mister Smith's back to him."

"Why would you be doing that?" Roan asked. "Let the law take care of him. No doubt, he'll be hanging."

"And he might not, too. If he gets out of this, he'll go on notching his gun butt."

Bino laughed loudly and buckled his gunbelt around his hips.

"Ain't that much difference between you and me, Hilton. We both kill for high money."

Hilton grunted. "There's a big difference, Bino. *You* are a young whelp who thinks you're a full-grown lobo — with fangs. You ready? Or would you rather crawfish?"

Hilton backed up until about twenty-five feet separated him from his adversary. Steppe and his crew, along with Ben, crowded against the far wall. Roan edged behind the bar in back of Bino Smith. From what Hilton had told him about Bino, Roan assumed the young gunfighter was plenty fast. Da's voice drew forth from his memory, "Me boy, always remember, a frightened or angry man doesn't have all his wits about him." He fixed his gaze on the albino. "However this turns out, Mister Smith, you need to be knowing that if you put Thax Hilton down, I'll put a bullet in your spine."

Steppe pushed away from the wall. "You dirty mick bastard!"

"Stay your ground, Azle Steppe," Roan warned.

Traces of red blotched Bino's pale cheeks. A drop of sweat appeared beneath one sideburn and rolled down his jawline. "Never mind, Steppe," he said, keeping his tone steady. "I'll get them both." He crouched, glaring at Hilton.

"Crawfish hell, I'm faster than you —"

And he was. He drew his own gun and aimed before Hilton cleared leather. But Bino's left hand wasn't as fast as his right. The heel of his hand barely touched the hammer when the bullet from Hilton's gun slammed him off his feet. Bino fell, spread-eagled, on his back. Blood spurted from a hole in the hollow of his throat.

No one spoke for several seconds. Finally, one of the men said, "Good God, I didn't figure anybody could outdraw Bino Smith. Whooee!"

Lank moaned. "You gonna get me a doc or you gonna let me bleed to death?"

"There'll be time for that soon enough," Roan said. "When you're locked safe in jail, we'll send somebody to look at your arm."

"You're not taking *me* to jail," Azle Steppe hissed. "No damn Irish scum or nigger bastard has that authority. Those tin badges don't mean anything."

Roan laid the rifle on the bar, reached out for Steppe and grabbed his shirt front. His fist landed flush on the rancher's jaw with a loud crack. Steppe whipped around and did a belly flop across the table behind him.

Steppe's legs were as malleable as melting tallow when the rancher slowly slid off the table to the floor.

Roan retrieved his rifle. Hilton stood nearby, grinning.

"I've been wanting to do that for years," Roan said, and returned Hilton's grin.

"Understandable." Hilton motioned to Steppe's men. "Pick him up. There's a horse tank out front. Let's go." He opened the door and stepped outside.

Roan waited until the last two men dragged Steppe past him. "Ben, I'll be sending a couple men after Bino Smith," he said. "Put those guns in a safe place. The sheriff will be wanting them tomorrow."

Closing the door behind him, he left the bar. A smile creased his face. Ben Shay looked more than relieved. Roan would bet as soon as they were out of sight, the bartender would have two or twenty samples of his own liquor stock.

Chapter Sixteen

Roan slept fitfully that night. If news of Azle Steppe's arrest reached the Double S or Q-C ranches, Steppe's men might try a raid on the jail.

"You think the townsfolk will help us, should we need them?" Roan asked, not once but five times throughout the night.

Each time, Hilton shrugged, looked hopeful, then doubtful, then hopeful again. "It's a crap shoot," he said finally.

The long night ended without incident. At mid-morning, Roan went back to the cells. He couldn't keep the tormenting tone out of his voice when he asked, "Where would Mister Tanner be, Azle Steppe? We expected him and your hired thugs during the night."

"My men will be here all right. I can assure you of that. You Irish bastard, you won't get away with this."

"Aye, it could be you're right, but there'll be a sight less men of your caliber around, maybe even yourself, before we fail. Right now, though, Mister Steppe, I'll be asking again about Jake Tanner."

Steppe glared and shrugged. "On a wild-goose chase obviously. After Hilton saved your ass the last time we saw you, we heard the wolf had attacked you and Hilton took you to the Dakota reservation. They said you were dying. I found out different after Tanner went to check on the story."

"Out there to shoot at me, wouldn't you be meaning, Mister Steppe?"

"Whatever it was, McCrae, we learned you were alive and ugly as ever. You still are — for the time being. Where was it you disappeared to?"

Roan laughed. "Your informant wasn't only wrong about me dying, he was wrong about some other facts as well. It was a grizzly did me harm, not me wolf friend. I stayed at the reservation for a good while."

"You weren't there when Tanner went back."

"And when was that?"

"Three, four days ago." Steppe smiled, an evil, sinister smile. "Tanner's got an obsession about you and that wolf. He's been telling everybody you'd be dead when he went after you this time. Too bad he was wrong."

"Aye, too bad for you, Mister Steppe." He returned to the marshal's office, his thoughts remaining on Tanner. The man had courage, though not enough sense to be afraid of that which was worthy of fear. Some innocent person was likely to be hurt if Tanner tried to force him to tell of Roan's whereabouts. It might even be Tula Moon. He couldn't let that happen. When Tanner went looking for him again, Roan would make certain the two of them found each other.

At noon, Roan crossed the street to buy meals for the prisoners as well as for Hilton and himself.

One look at the stack of orders ahead of his and he decided he had more than enough time to keep his word to Tula. "I'll be back for me answer," he had told her. He hurried toward the stairs.

A twinge of regret washed over him as he passed Warren Quade's room. He stopped, wondering if he should look in on the man who had been his friend for a while, decided not to and took another step toward Tula's quarters.

From inside Quade's room came a stream of curses and the sound of something heavy thunking against a hard object.

Roan knocked, then called, "Are you all right, Warren Quade? Would you be needing anything?"

"Come in, Roan," Quade answered, not in his usual resonant timbre, but huskily and a little out of breath.

Roan opened the door, found the rancher dressed and sitting on the edge of the bed, huffing with exertion. One foot was booted. The other was not. The second boot rested against the wall several feet away. Quade regarded it.

"What the devil do you think you're about, Warren Quade?" Roan asked. "Why have you left your bed and you barely healing from the bullet?"

Quade struggled for a breath. "That's the same question I've asked myself these last few minutes, Roan." He leaned back, supporting his weight on his arms. His breathing slowed before he continued, "Hell, I've been laying here thinking what a son-of-a-bitch I was yesterday. I decided I had to find you and tell you —"

He straightened and pointed toward the empty boot. "Trouble is, I'm too damned weak to put my own boots on. How about a hand, Roan?"

Roan laughed. Instead of helping slip Quade's foot into the remaining boot, he lifted his friend's other foot and removed the boot from it. "If you'll just lie yourself down here, me friend, and rest awhile." He punched the pillow and waited while Quade settled himself.

"After awhile, you'll get up and walk around the room a couple of times. In a few days you'll be getting your strength back, but this day you'll not be making it down the stairs much less across the street."

Quade's expression was that of a child caught stealing a pie from the windowsill. "I know you're right, Roan. I just wish you weren't. I feel so — so damned helpless. And that's what the whole thing was about yesterday. I hate being helpless. A confined man has too much time to think — to brood."

"Aye, I've tasted a whit of such confinement meself."

"I convinced myself you were to blame for the way Tula has been acting."

"In truth, Warren Quade, am I not to blame?"

Quade studied on the question. "I guess you are, but not deliberately. I was certain you and she had —"

"You were wrong, me friend, dead wrong. It's not me intention to make Tula Moon me consort. I'll be making her me wife."

Quade winced as the impact of Roan's words hit him. "I think I should tell you something else, Roan. I'm sorry about the things I said to you. I ask you to forgive me for them. But —"

"There's no forgiveness needed," Roan said. "And I don't like 'buts' such as the one you spoke hanging in the air between us. Speak your mind, Warren Quade."

"I intend to fight for Tula. We both love her and, as you said, you're a man who doesn't like to lose. Neither do I. I'll do everything I can to keep her with me."

"And I'll be battling you at every turn."

"Fair enough." Quade extended his hand and waited until Roan gripped it firmly. "Can we be friends with Tula between us?"

"We are friends. And friends we'll remain. Tula Moon will be making up her own mind which of us she wants. There'll be no quarrel between us whichever she chooses."

Roan moved to the door, opened it part way, and said, "The sheriff will be here sometime this evening. He'll be talking to you before we leave."

"Leave?"

"Aye. We'll be taking your ranch back for you tonight."

"God, I wish I could go with you."

"Aye. I wish it as well, but there'll be aplenty

of us." He backed out of the door, his hand raised in farewell.

"Be careful," Quade called.

Roan turned just in time to see Tula standing in her doorway. He hurried to her, pushed her back into the room and closed the door.

"What do you think you're doing, Roan McCrae?"

"What does it look like, lass? I came for me answer like I said." He tried to pull her close, but she backed away.

She dropped into a nearby chair. "My answer hasn't changed. I prayed to Wakan Tanka to keep you safe. When you go to the ranch tonight, I will pray again."

"And when it's all done, you'll be coming with me." It was not a question, but a statement. He had told Warren Quade the truth. He hated to lose a fight, especially one that would send him back to the lonely life he had lived since Katie's death.

"No, Roan. I'll stay with Warren. It is the way of my people. Will you never understand?"

"It's this I'm understanding, lass. I want you for me own."

"I asked that we never speak of this again. But I will speak this and no more. My wish is the same as yours, that we be together, but it's better that we die apart than to be joined in the anger of the spirits."

"It's a foolishness you believe, I'm thinking, Tula Moon."

"If I leave Warren when he needs me most, I would be defying all the Wakanda. Their wrath would follow me. It has always been the way of my people. Betray a friend and one betrays Wakan Tanka. One will live forever in torment."

"Maybe it's a torment you've already earned."

"How?"

"By learning in the white man's schools, living his way. Do you not be thinking that a bit wrong? Do your *People* not frown on anything to do with the white man?" He had not meant to sound so derisive, but he had contained anger as long as he could. It had built since his confrontation with Quade the day before and now reached a crest from which he was helpless to descend.

When she spoke, her words were cold and edged with quiet anger. "It's best we don't talk of the ways of The People, Roan. You will never understand. Nor will you try."

"If you'd be kind enough to explain it to me, then perhaps —"

"I wanted the education for myself. No one has been hurt by it. Certainly not my people. If anything, they have benefited. The spirits look kindly upon all that helps their people."

"Then is it that you can change some of the ways of your tribe, but others must remain as they were? You can pick and choose as may benefit yourself?"

"Some of our ways have changed, that's true. Living on the reservation, under the white man's

206

law, did that for us. We were forced to change. But our religion, the cycle of our lives — that never changes."

"I understand."

"No, I don't think you do, Roan. My beliefs, my ways are who I am. How can I change them?"

"It seems to me you're mightily afraid of bringing hurt to one person, that being me friend Warren Quade. And you're not caring a whit how much you hurt another. Trouble is, you're hurting both." He turned toward the door, his hand on the knob.

"Roan, wait! Somehow I must make you understand how I feel, why it can't be as you wish it to be."

Roan opened the door. "Be telling it to Warren Quade, lass. Sit with him awhile and talk. Tell him the ways of your people. Maybe he'll have some answers for you. I don't."

He slammed the door behind him, his wrath yielding to growing heartbreak. Must he spend the rest of his life alone? Maybe Tula was right. He had angered *somebody's* gods and the punishment could be more than he could stand.

So immersed had he been in his own troubles that Roan forgot he had gone for lunches. He stood at the front door to the jail before he remembered. With an oath, he turned and strode across to the hotel cafe.

Time crawled that afternoon. Finally, at four o'clock, Sheriff Tom Cordale arrived with five deputies and Marshal Tindal. "This here's Roan McCrae and —" Tindal began.

"I know Thaxter Hilton, but what are you doing wearing a badge, Thax? You turned mine down last year. I'll wager mine paid more."

Hilton's dark eyes regarded the sheriff's heavy jowls, the bushy brows shadowing gray eyes. "I just wasn't ready then, Tom. Besides, Roan and I only took this job temporarily while the marshal went for you. We'll stay until this matter is settled."

Tindal listened, his hands clenching and unclenching, as nervous as a naked man walking through a cactus field.

A wide grin on his face, Thax winked at Roan. "By the way, Marshal, we got that chore done you left for us."

"What chore? Oh . . . you did?" He cleared his throat. "You got Bino Smith and Steppe back there in the cells?"

"We've got Steppe and four of his gun hands."

"And Bino Smith?"

"Smith didn't see his way clear to accept our invitation, Marshal."

Tension gathered in Tindal's expression. Suddenly he exploded, "My God! He escaped. You let Bino Smith escape." His eyes bulged. He looked back and forth from Roan to Hilton. "You let him escape. You gotta find him. Gotta bring him in. Kill him if you have to." He whirled toward the sheriff. "Bino Smith, Sheriff. He's a killer. He's —"

Roan stifled a laugh. Beside him, Hilton spluttered.

He jabbed his elbow into Hilton's ribs. Thax immediately turned his back to the Marshal, his shoulders heaving with laughter.

"It's all right, Mister Tindal," Roan blurted. "We know where Bino Smith is."

"You do? You gotta go get him. Kill him if you have to."

"Well, Marshal, sir, that might be a wee whit difficult for us to do. You see, he's reposing over in Doc Weller's back parlor."

"Oh, good, go get him. He's . . . what? What did you say? Back room? Oh. He's dead?" His shoulders slumped in relief.

"Aye, he's dead, Marshal Tindal. He drew on Mister Hilton here. It was a mistake."

Tindal eyed Hilton, beginning with the holstered gun and traveling upward. He squared his shoulders and hitched his pants. "Outdrew him, did you? That's good. Very good. Good work, men. Saved the courts the expense of hanging him, I'd say. Wouldn't you say so, Sheriff Cordale?"

Cordale opened his mouth to speak, but Tindal cut him off. "You wanted to talk with Azle Steppe. Follow me."

Grabbing a ring of keys off his desk, he headed for the back.

Cordale followed until he got to the door. He halted and winked at Roan and Hilton. A grin spread across his wide mouth. He shook his head and wagged his finger at them before he closed the door behind him.

Roaring laughter erupted in the jail office.

Three hours past dark, Roan led the small group of lawmen to the offside of a designated hill west of the Q-C Ranch quarters. Dim light from the sliver of moon revealed no evidence of Falcon and his braves, nor could Roan see any sign that they had been there.

"Think he'll show?" Cordale asked.

"He'll show all right," Hilton replied. "A four-mule drag team couldn't keep him from something like this."

Only a couple of minutes later, a voice behind Hilton asked, "Ho, Buffalo Soldier. What kept you?"

Startled, Hilton whirled, his hand reaching for his gun.

Falcon laughed and accepted the bear hug Hilton wrapped him in. "Damn sneaking Indian. I ought to peel your hide for that." He turned and introduced the brave to Cordale and his deputies.

"McCrae said you'd have your band of men with you," Cordale said. "I guess I should have brought my other two deputies along."

Roan interrupted. "It's a certainty, Sheriff, Falcon's men will be close by."

"Yes," Hilton agreed. "Call them, Falcon."

Falcon cupped his hands around his mouth. The soft hoot of *bue*, the owl, floated through the stillness. Like phantoms from a mist, Falcon's warriors quietly surrounded Roan and his companions.

"Great galloping ghosts," exclaimed one of the deputies. "Where the hell were they?"

"There." Falcon laughed softly.

"Yeah," Cordale said, his eyes widening in awe. "There. How in the hell the cavalry ever whipped the Sioux is a wonder to me."

"They didn't *whip* us," Falcon replied. "The Sioux would kill one yellow leg, but two took his place. Their tactics didn't defeat my people. Their numbers did. Our fathers saw the futility and finally surrendered."

"By damn," another deputy said, "you talk like you been educated."

Falcon nodded. "I went to the white man's school. How about you? Do you know the Sioux tongue or anything of our culture?"

"Well, no." The deputy shook his head. "Never had no reason to."

"There you have it." Falcon shrugged. "We had to learn your ways to survive. It's a white man's world."

The sheriff studied the band of braves crowded around him. "Do these others understand English?"

"Most of them."

"Good. I think we better consider our strategy. There are enough of us, I think, so's we can take this place back with very little shooting. Hopefully, none at all."

"That doesn't sound very exciting," Falcon complained.

The sheriff smiled. "I hate the sight of blood."

After an hour of planning, selecting exactly what each man's job was to be, Cordale broke up the session.

"You men can rest or sleep — whatever you want — until the hour we agreed on. Two hours before dawn."

Chapter Seventeen

They built a small fire beneath a rock outcropping. Sheriff Cordale produced coffee from his supply pack and, soon, the smell of the strong brew wafted over the area.

Roan accepted a steaming cup, then moved over to sit with his back against a large boulder. The sheriff's plan churned through his mind. It ought to work without a hitch. Such a simple plan. One that depended on the hour when all who were on the ranch would be sound asleep.

Get the guards first. Quick and quiet would be needed for that. Most of the hired guns would be sleeping in the bunkhouse. Eighteen men volunteered to take care of that spot, most of them Sioux warriors led by Cordale and Thax Hilton.

The ranch house had four bedrooms, one on the main floor, three upstairs. Roan, Falcon and the rest of the men would be responsible for securing the house.

Roan smiled at the thought. Every man on the Q-C would be awakened to find the barrel of a cocked gun pressed between his eyes.

Falcon seated himself beside Roan. "Jake Tanner rode out to the reservation a couple days ago."

"Aye, it was Azle Steppe told me. Said Tanner was looking for meself and Patch. Did the scudder hurt anyone?"

"No, he left after they told him you had taken

the wolf to the far country."

"Good. It's me hope he's fast asleep in the main house tonight." A grin creased Roan's face, deepening the craggy shadows cast by the dancing flames. "It'd be me pleasure to waken the man with me gun stuck up his nose."

"Hi yi." Falcon chuckled. "I want to be there when you do it. I can just see those narrow set eyes of his bulging so wide they'll crowd his face for room." He pounded the ground and nearly choked trying to stifle his laughter.

Roan muffled his own mirth and jabbed an elbow into Falcon's ribs. "You're indeed something else, friend Falcon Claw. You bring me laughter each time I'm with you. But about Jake Tanner. He's no coward. You need to know that."

"Maybe not. But damn! I'd think something like having the end of your nose stuck into a gun barrel would have the piss running down the leg of the bravest man."

Roan did his best to hide laughter. "It's right you may be, Falcon. Otherwise we might have to be shooting the sorry bastard."

Quiet fell over the two of them. Most of the others sat around talking in low tones, too nervous to sleep. Hilton spoke for a while with Sheriff Cordale and his deputies, but finally came over and joined Roan and Falcon.

"You intend going back up north again when all this is over, Roan?" he asked.

"It's me plan, Thaxter Hilton, but I'll be trying

first to find a buyer for me ranch."

"You're not coming back here?"

"I think I'd like to touch the old sod again. I'm hoping to sail to Ireland."

Hilton's face mirrored his disappointment. Aloud he said, "A free man has to do the thing that makes him happiest."

"Aye. And it's me fondest wish you two will go with me."

Falcon grinned and answered with a vigorous nod. "I would like that very much. But I'm afraid the U.S. government wouldn't see it our way."

"And you, Mister Hilton, will you be going along?"

"Thanks, Roan, for asking, but I'd be like a polar bear in the Sahara in a foreign country. I'll stay on with Warren Quade until he hires a new crew and breaks them in. Cordale's asked me to come to work for him. I'm taking him up on the offer."

"It's time, men," Cordale interrupted. "Falcon, you got your boys ready?"

"We're always ready." He waved his hand. In less than a minute, he and Gray Fox, along with three other young Sioux warriors, crawled over the hilltop and out of sight.

Tension gripped Roan and, if he could believe the terse comments and lack of humor in the attitudes of the others, the same tension gripped his companions. If a shot sounded now, the plan would be ruined. An all-out battle would ensue. Men would die, some of them his friends. One of them might be him.

As minutes passed, tension mounted. Suddenly, a scraping sound followed by a soft grunt called Roan's attention to the hilltop. A body rolled down the side of the incline and came to rest at Roan's feet. A second later, another followed, then three more. All were unconscious, bound and gagged.

Cordale's voice seemed to boom through the quiet. "You! Deputy Jenkins! You stay here and guard these five. The rest of you, follow me."

He led them over the hill and down the opposite slope. As they reached the ranch yard, they separated into two groups. Roan and Falcon had eight others with them. They moved silently to the back door of the main ranch house.

Inside, almost total darkness enveloped them as they crowded onto the porch. Roan struck a match and opened the door into the kitchen. A lamp in a wall bracket gave off a dim light. The kitchen was filthy. He remembered how neat, how spotlessly clean Tula Moon kept it.

The men passed through into the large parlor, lit by wall lamps. Roan shook his head at the clutter. Whiskey bottles, dirty dishes and soiled clothing littered the floor and furnishings where, it seemed so long ago, he sat and talked with Warren Quade surrounded by the beauty of the room.

At the stairway, Roan pointed out the three bedrooms and whispered, "If you can't see, light a lamp, but be at the ready. Like the Sheriff said, it's mean bastards these be. They'll likely go for their guns. If they do, you shoot to kill. Are you all understanding what I say?"

He waited for their nods before motioning them to ascend the steps. To Falcon, he whispered, "I'm thinking Jake Tanner is likely downstairs in the master bedroom."

Falcon smiled, his rifle cradled in the crook of his arm. He rubbed his hands together in a sign of eagerness. Roan swallowed a chuckle and led Falcon down the hallway. Silently, he slid the door open.

Falcon stepped in ahead of Roan, the rifle now gripped securely in one hand, a knife gleaming in the other.

Roan struck a second match, lit the wall lamp and turned around. Surprise wouldn't begin to describe his state of mind when he realized this hadn't been Warren Quade's room, as he had supposed. Obviously, it belonged to Tula Moon.

Two men sprawled on the bed. Neither of the filthy rakesails was Tanner. The smell of sweat mingled with stale whiskey filled the room.

Instantly, Roan's temper flared. Those hellborn bastards defiled the bed on which Tula should lie.

He cast a glace at Falcon, reading in the Indian's face the same revulsion he felt.

"Slithering pit vipers," Falcon muttered. "Maybe we should pull their fangs."

Roan nodded. "It's the same thing I've been thinking, friend Falcon." He reached down and grasped the dirty undershirt of the one nearest to him.

The outlaw's eyes sprang open. "What the — ?"

Roan yanked him out of the bed.

"What's goin' — ?" His words halted when Roan smashed his face against the nearest wall. His legs folded beneath him and he crumpled into a heap on the floor.

Falcon held the other man, who was quite short, by the ankles and bounced him up and down like a butter churn, his head beating a rhythmic tattoo against the hardwood floor. Falcon laughed each time his captive shouted, "Hey! Hey! Hey!"

The "heying" stopped when the tat-tat became a loud crack against the door facing. Falcon dumped the limp form into the hall.

Roan lifted the unconscious man he had dealt with and held him at arm's length as though the stinking form was something to be reviled. "Do you think, Falcon, we should dispose of this garbage with the other?"

Falcon nodded, retrieved his rifle and followed as Roan dragged the gunman out of the room.

Roan dropped both men at the stairway.

The quiet was shattered by the blast of a gun on the second floor.

Two steps at a time, Roan bounded up the stairs and stood ready on the landing. Two of the rooms had already been secured. The outlaws were lined up along the balcony with their faces turned toward the wall. One of Falcon's braves pointed out the end bedroom. Another young Indian held his gun at the ready as they crept cautiously down the hallway. The smell of cordite hung heavy in the air.

Just as they reached the door, Gray Fox stepped out dragging a body. "This one not so drunk," he said. "Reach for gun, but not quick." Blood oozed from a neat hole in the middle of the man's forehead.

Slowly, the prisoners marched down to the main floor where they sat back to back in the middle of the room. Tanner wasn't among them. "I'll check the bunkhouse," Roan said.

He went through the kitchen and along the outside hall. As he opened the door, he was surprised to find the yard brightly lit. Holding burning torches, the sheriff and his men stood in two parallel rows. The outlaws were ushered between the ranks. Most were still in their underwear, hands reaching toward the night sky.

Roan stepped back inside the ranch house. "Bring these scudders on out," he told Falcon. "Everything out there is well under control."

Was-ma-got-tu," Falcon grumbled. "The boys and I were hoping for a little more excitement."

"Now, 'tis a shame, friend Falcon, that you didn't get a good fight. It was me wish as well." Roan grinned. "Do you think it's time we retrieved the boys who didn't want to leave Tula Moon's bed?"

As they approached the stairway, both men were sitting up. Blood streaked their faces. One obviously had a broken nose and a cut on his mouth. The other displayed a sizable gash on his forehead. Roan went to the kitchen and returned with wet cloths. These he handed to the injured gunhands, saying, "Would you gentlemen be so kind as to get to your feet and come along with us?"

They made no effort to comply.

Falcon kicked at the leg of the one nearest to him. "Let's go!" he ordered.

Outside, they shoved the two toward the others. Roan hailed Hilton who stood nearby. "Did you have any trouble?" he asked.

"Not a whisper," Hilton replied. "The damn fools must have had a party. Most of them are still falling down drunk. How about you? I heard a gunshot."

"Only one gave us a wee problem. Seems he thought it was a whit early to get up. Gray Fox arranged for him to rest kind of permanent." He glanced toward the grouped outlaws. "Have you seen Jake Tanner among them?"

"No. I looked for him. I figured he would be in the main house."

Falcon joined them. Roan told him, "Tanner's absent tonight. Do you suppose he might have returned to the reservation?"

Frowning, Falcon studied the question. "If he did, it had to be after midday yesterday when we left there."

"Maybe we can ask Cordale to question these blackguards," Hilton suggested.

Cordale and Gray Fox stood together talking with two of the Sheriff's deputies. As Roan approached, Cordale said, "All right, go get them saddled, but make damn sure they're watered and grained. It'll be a full day's ride." To the others, he said, "Boys, there's no place here big enough to hold this bunch. I'm taking them on in to the penitentiary at Deer Lodge."

"I've been wondering what you intended to do with this many," Hilton admitted. "That answers it, but we're minus one, Tom."

"Who's that?"

"Jake Tanner. He's foreman of the Double S spread."

"Maybe that's where he is then — at the Double S."

Roan interrupted. "It's possible you're right, Sheriff, but we'll be wanting to question this scurvy crew to be sure."

Cordale raised a hand toward the outlaws. "Have at it."

Hilton spoke to the one nearest him, calling him by name. "Decker, do you know Jake Tanner?"

"Hell, yes, who don't?" The reply was sullen, but the others laughed as though they enjoyed the game their cohort played.

"Then maybe you'll be kind enough to tell us where Tanner is?" Roan suggested.

Decker gestured toward a tall, slope-shouldered man a few feet away. "Ask him."

"Ah, yes, Mister Quince," Hilton said. "What

221

about it, Quince? Tanner tell you where he was going?"

Quince stared at Hilton's gleaming face for a long time before he shrugged and answered, "Hell with 'im. I don't owe the sonofabitch nothin'. Prob'ly knowed the law was comin' an' that's the reason he cut out."

"Cut out to where?"

"Don't know exactly, Hilton. Whole thing sounded kinda stupid to me. Said somethin' about goin' up north." He shrugged. "Don't know where, just north. Some Irish bastard up there had a pet wolf. Tanner said he was gonna kill both the sonsabitches."

Falcon motioned with his head for Roan and the other two to move with him a few feet away. "Why would Tanner do that? Go north," he asked. "He has no way of knowing where that cabin is. Not unless he's as good as the brothers at tracking."

"He is that good, Falcon," Hilton said. "Believe me. You and Roan left tracks up to that cabin. Only a hard rain can keep Tanner from following them."

"Damn," Falcon muttered.

"I'll be taking me leave right now," Roan said, his tone filled with anxiety. "If Jake Tanner even catches a wee glimpse of Patch, he'll kill him."

"I wouldn't worry too much, Roan," Falcon told him. "That wolf will smell Tanner. There's no way he'll let himself be seen unless, of course, brother wolf *wants* to be seen."

"Aye, I'm praying to the saints you be right, Falcon Claw." Roan offered his hand to the Sheriff.

"Wait just a minute," Cordale said. "Roan, you can't leave now. I'm going to need help getting these yahoos to the penitentiary."

"Me friend Patch needs help more."

Cordale shook his head, his brow creased with concern. "I don't understand. You're going north to help a wolf? North where?"

"Saskatchewan."

"My God, man. That far? And to save a wolf? Wolves and men are bitter enemies in cattle country."

Falcon put up his hand for silence. "This is a very crazy Irishman, Sheriff, and Patch is a very special wolf." A smile tugged at the corners of his mouth.

Hilton joined the conversation. "Ever see a wolf tear into a grizzly?"

"Are you crazy?" Cordale looked back and forth between Falcon and Hilton. "No wolf would fight a —"

"Patch did," Hilton insisted.

"You saw him do it?"

"Didn't have to. I saw Roan, half dead from the bear's attack. He told me Patch saved his life."

"That true, Roan?" Cordale turned in disbelief.

" 'Tis true. Patch is me friend, me brother. Had it not been for him, I'd be buried beneath the sod in that lonely wood."

"But Saskatchewan."

"Aye, and I'll be bringing Jake Tanner to you unless he forces me back to the wall and I have to kill him."

"I hope that's not the case, Roan. My thanks for your help here. Without you and these boys, this job would have been pure-D hell."

Roan nodded. "And will I be seeing you again, Thax Hilton?" he asked.

"I'll be here when you get back. My money's on you, but be damned careful. Jake Tanner's a sneaky bastard. You well know that."

"Aye, that I do." Roan made ready to say his farewells to Falcon, but the young Indian stopped him.

"I'm going with you."

"They'll be needing you here."

"But Tanner —"

Roan grasped Falcon's shoulders. "Have a wee whit of faith in me, Falcon. I'll handle Mister Tanner. You well know our brothers won't be taking orders from a white man. Sheriff Cordale needs you until these scudders are in jail."

Falcon breathed in the morning air. Finally, he said, "All right, but if you aren't back within seven days, we'll be there on the tenth day." He hesitated for a moment before adding, "I'll give you my promise, Roan, should Jake Tanner get lucky, there won't be a place on Wakan Tanka's green earth where he can hide."

Roan's eyes misted. He fought the lump that rose in his throat. "You speak like the true brother you are, friend Falcon. I'll be seeing the lot of you."

He embraced the Indian, turned and ran toward the hill. On the other side, the dun would be fresh and ready to run.

Chapter Eighteen

The first trip to the north country took Roan and Falcon over a week, but they had been in no hurry and they were slowed by the travois with Shadow and her pups.

Returning to Buckhorn to help Warren Quade had been a different matter. There was need to get back quickly. The traveling time was cut in half.

Roan felt the same immediacy now. He would do as he and the brothers did when they returned to Buckhorn — allow an hour every so often for sleep and to let the horse rest and graze.

He followed his and Falcon's return trail as he knew Tanner would. Within an hour he found the tracks which assured him Tanner was ahead of him. They weren't over twenty-four hours old if he was any judge. Big "if." His abilities as a tracker were limited. He tried not to regret having refused Falcon's offer to accompany him. Falcon and Gray Fox both could read tracks. But then, why place either of them, his adopted brothers, in the danger he would face?

He shook his head. Hell, these tracks might be half again as old as he estimated.

If his first guess was right he would catch up with Tanner before he reached the cabin. Even if he was wrong about the tracks, he had a chance to get ahead. Tanner had to follow them. Roan didn't. He already knew the way and was in a lot more hurry than Tanner would be.

He tried not to think of Patch in life-threatening danger. Each time the thought crept forward, he shoved it back.

Three days and as many nights later, he found his initial judgment wrong. He topped the mountain ridge which descended to the lake. As he rode downward, he saw the dim glow of a lamp through the cabin window across the water.

But suppose Tanner wasn't inside the cabin. Suppose he was outside looking in the direction of the ridge. With the moon so full and bright, it was possible he could see Roan coming along the trail.

He nudged the dun's flanks and held his breath until his mount walked along the lake's shoreline. Halfway to the cabin, Roan halted and dismounted, tying the reins securely to the nearest tree. He pulled his rifle from the boot, cocked it and crept cautiously up to the cabin.

Standing a couple feet back, he peered through the window, but the light was too dim and the window too dirty. A lump beneath the blankets on one of the bunks could be Tanner. He worked his way carefully toward the back door, which was closer to the bunks.

Just as he lifted his foot to step onto the back porch, a low guttural laugh stopped him cold. From behind, Tanner's voice ordered, "Don't move, Irish, or I'll split your spine where you stand."

Roan's obedience brought another evil chuckle.

"Damn, would you look how lucky I been tonight. So purty out I decided to take me a little walk. Seen you coming off the ridge up there so I ran inside and fixed that bunk so's you'd think I was in it. Smart, huh?" He laughed again.

Like he was carved from stone, Roan stood rigid, controlling his breathing so he wouldn't give even the slightest impression of movement. Stay yourself, he admonished silently, and the phrase presented itself in his mind — stay *dead still.*

"I sort of figured you'd come around the back since the bunks is closer to that door," Tanner continued. "Smart again."

Tanner had him and, without doubt, intended to kill him. Right soon, if he knew anything about the big foreman. He had to keep Tanner talking, had to locate his exact position from the sound of his voice.

"Aye, Mister Tanner, you're a smart one all right. When did you get here?"

"This afternoon. When I found out you'd gone away with whoever was here, I almost left. Decided to see could I find that damn wolf first though." Low and mean, the laughter erupted again.

"And did you do that? Did you find him?"

"Found the sonofabitch all right. Want to see him? He's laying in that clearing back of here. Blew the calf-killing bastard's head clean off." Another sinister chuckle. "Now, Irish, it's your —"

Roan's blood froze in his veins, but his mind

kept working. His hearing, keened by years of tracking wolves, had picked up Tanner's location. He whirled and pulled the trigger on the rifle.

Before he had time to see if his bullet had hit its mark, he heard a low growl and Tanner's surprised, "What the —" A split second later, Tanner's terrified scream tore through the night and his gun exploded, sending a shower of sparks from its barrel.

Roan expected the slug to slam him backwards. When it didn't, he stared in transfixed horror. Tanner's scream died in a gurgling sputter. His massive body fell to the ground, highlighted by a strip of bright moonlight, his legs kicking in the last throes of life.

Patch straddled him, thrashing him back and forth, his fangs fastened onto Tanner's throat.

At first Roan wasn't certain what had taken place. When he was, he called, "No, Patch. No!"

The only response was another low growl. The wolf released Tanner and regarded Roan. Tanner's blood soaked into the fur around his mouth. He drew back his lips and snarled a warning.

"Patch, me friend, have you forgotten so soon? 'Tis me, don't you remember?" He snapped his fingers sharply. "Come, Patch."

The wolf snarled again, moved a few steps backward and stopped in a pool of moonlight. He sank back on his haunches. Roan watched as Patch raised his head and emitted a long mournful howl.

From far in the distance came an answering call.

Now Roan understood. He seated himself on the ground and rested his arms across his knees. "You finally know, don't you, Brother Wolf? You've finally realized man is your enemy. Well, not meself. I'll be your friend for as long as you care to have me. Jake Tanner wasn't. By the saints, he'd have killed us both, Patch. Faith, it's twice now you've saved me life and it was me come to save yours."

Patch remained seated. He looked like a statue, so still Roan could hardly tell he was breathing.

"Me boy, I'm praying it wasn't your mate Tanner shot. I'm thinking that'd be near impossible though. She's smart like you, too smart for the likes of Tanner."

Patch cocked his head, watching Roan, listening to him. Suddenly, he sent forth another mournful howl.

"I know. I know. You'll be going away. Well, go far, me friend, far to the north. Take your family out of man's reach. It was me thinking this place would be far enough, but I was wrong. Go where your kind can live long and peaceful with no fear of man."

Patch rose, and stood for several seconds, his attention fixed on Roan. With two sharp barks, he turned and ran.

"So long, little brother. May those who guard you do it well," Roan called after him, feeling the lump in his throat give way to tears of loss.

As he had been so many times in his life, he was alone again. He got to his feet and walked to the clearing. He had to satisfy himself the dead wolf wasn't Patch's mate.

Even at a distance, he knew the animal was one he had never seen before. It was young, maybe two years old, judging from size. Roan approached the center of the clearing where the wolf laid. It was a male. He could only suppose it had satisfied Tanner's brutal ego to think this little whelp could be the great beast Roan loved.

He swung back toward the cabin. A chore awaited him. Burying Tanner. Burying him deep. Perhaps he could bury his memories as well.

A distant howl was borne along the soft breeze. Patch. Roan waited for an answer. There was none.

He tried to smile. Patch and his family were together. But Roan faced a lot of empty tomorrows. True, he had settled the matter with Jake Tanner. But Patch was gone, maybe forever. So was Katie, his first love. His second true love — Tula Moon — was lost to him as well.

He swiped at the dampness in his eyes and told himself it was mist coming in from the lake. So tired he was of lonely tears.

Roan hadn't realized how exhausted he was until he lay down that night. He fell asleep immediately despite the terror earlier and slept well into the next day, waking only long enough to eat a bite, then slept again, all night and far into morning. When he awoke he felt refreshed. He headed for the stream Falcon had introduced him to. He caught four fair-sized trout in less than thirty minutes.

"So," he said aloud. "Today will be fish day. And tomorrow? Maybe deer and rabbit the next." He glanced around as though he felt someone might have heard him talking to himself.

He was right about the deer. In mid-morning on the following day, he cornered a young two-pronged buck. Venison steaks would satisfy his palate for at least six meals. After that, he shot a couple of squirrels and trapped a rabbit.

But even those foods he savored tasted like sawdust without someone to share them with. Patch would have loved the venison. Tula would have made the squirrels into a delicacy as she had so many times when he visited the Q-C.

He tried to fill his time. Refusing to allow the loneliness to consume him, he swam and basked in the sun. But he couldn't shut out the desolation. On day seven, the memories set in and wouldn't leave.

He went for a ride because he had nothing better to occupy his time. At the edge of the woods, he spotted a grizzly. "And wouldn't it be the way of the saints," he said, "that you and meself would meet when I least need company from the likes of you?"

He leveled his rifle, fired one shot and found the action enough to send the beast packing. Roan watched him retreat, but instead of seeing this bear he remembered another — it seemed so long ago — and Patch running behind, periodically nipping at the fat rear. The vision stayed with him most of that day.

Sleep didn't come so easily the next two nights. Near dawn, he drifted off into a restless slumber. Thoughts of Tula filled his mind. He saw her beauty and remembered the soft warmth of her mouth, the smell of her, the throaty sound of her voice and low, lilting laugh.

Only when he thought of their last parting — her words, the bitterness he felt afterward — could he sleep. But the sleep was filled with nightmares and he awoke exhausted.

On the tenth day, the day when Falcon had said he would come, Roan made a decision. When Falcon returned to the reservation, Roan would return with him. He would do as he had told Falcon and Hilton. He would sell his ranch and use the money for a ticket back to the green isle. Maybe there, with the vast distance separating him from Tula Moon, he could forget.

He walked along the lakeshore, climbed a mountain, tramped through the forest and across the wide valley to the east of the cabin. If Falcon didn't come, maybe he would be tired enough to sleep.

In late evening, he approached the lake from the east and saw the flames of a campfire and smoke billowing from the cabin chimney. "Must be me friend, Falcon, and perhaps, some of the Sioux brothers." His mood brightened a little.

He ran toward the site.

As he drew near, Falcon whooped and met him with a strong embrace. Falcon lifted him off the ground, laughing. When he let Roan down, he said, "By the love of Wakan Tanka, it is good to see you, my brother."

Roan wrapped an arm around the Indian's shoulder as they walked into the camp. " 'Tis a good feeling to see all me brothers," he said as he greeted Gray Fox and three other young Sioux braves.

Falcon handed him a cup of strong herbal tea and he seated himself among them. "You know, Falcon, you told the truth to me once when you said this was lonely country."

Falcon laughed. "You're ready to go back then?"

"Aye. When you go, I'll go also." He had no wish to remind his friends of the rest of his plan, that an ocean might soon lie between them. But they knew. He could see it in their faces.

"Did you find Tanner?" Falcon asked. "Did he come here?"

"Aye. But he won't be leaving. Ever."

"We are more pleased at that than we probably should be, Roan," Falcon said, smiling. "You always were dead center with a rifle."

"That may be true, Falcon Claw, but it wasn't meself who killed Tanner. It was Patch."

"And wolf brother?" Gray Fox asked. "He all right?"

Roan nodded. "He's fine, him and his mate,

but he took his family to safer ground, far north."

The Indians' faces were solemn.

"Wash-ta," Gray Fox said quietly. "He will be safe. Is the way of *Waka-ita*, mother of The People."

They sat in silence for a while. Roan sipped his tea, wondering how he could be with friends like Falcon and Gray Fox and the other brothers, yet all the while nurturing such desolation inside him.

Out in the tall pines a fox barked, breaking the spell. Falcon punched Gray Fox on the shoulder. "Your little brother calls."

Fox grunted. "He too little, too fast. Can no catch."

"True," Falcon replied, "and a whole lot handsomer, too."

The laughter managed only to make Roan feel more isolated, more lonely.

When the mirth quieted, Roan switched subjects. "You made it to the prison with the Double S men all right?"

"Fine, except for a couple of them. They tried to escape," Falcon said. "Didn't get far. Gray Fox saw to that."

"And Azle Steppe? He and his men?"

"The sheriff and his deputies took them to Deer Lodge. The brothers and I took Warren Quade and Tula back to the Q-C. Quade is getting along fine."

Roan stared into the fire, wanting to ask about Tula, afraid his voice would fail him if he did.

Falcon seemed to sense Roan's uneasiness. He laid his hand on his friend's shoulder. "The brothers and I made ourselves at home before you returned."

"I would expect no different," Roan told him.

"Gray Fox has some *to-ma-she* cooking on the hearth. Venison stew. Perhaps we should eat."

Roan nodded absently, the thought of food as distasteful now as it had been since he returned to the north country.

"And," Falcon continued, "maybe you can find us something a little stronger than tea to drink. We occasionally have a taste for — what does the white man think we call it? — fire water? You have anything like that in the cabin? We looked, but you've hidden the jug well if it's there."

Roan brightened a little. He hadn't thought of dulling the ache inside him with whiskey, but the idea appealed to him. If he got gloriously drunk, he would sleep without dreams. "Aye, Jake Tanner brought a supply with him. It's beneath the blankets on one of the bunks. I'll get it."

Roan hurried to the cabin. Tonight he would not think of Tula, or Patch or leaving the brothers forever. Tonight he would drink and forget.

As he opened the cabin door, the aroma of the stew reached his nostrils. His stomach rumbled in response. Maybe he was hungry, a little.

The sight by the hearth stopped him, wiping all thought from his mind. Tula stood by the fire, a pan in her hand. She wore a beaded buckskin

236

blouse and skirt. Beaded boots adorned her feet. Her hair was unbraided and hung like black silk far down her back, held away from her face by a white headband.

Roan drank in her beauty. Indeed, she was the loveliest creature he had ever seen.

She raised her head.

Roan saw the brightness in her eyes. His arms ached to hold her, but instead, he asked, "Why did you come here, Tula me girl?"

"To see you." Her voice was calm, but he detected the quaver in it.

"But why would you want to be seeing me after — ?"

"Because I love you. You are the light within me."

Roan held his breath. "For the love of the saints, lass, you told me that once before, then you ran away. I love you, too, but not for just a wee moment now and again. I love you for always." He shook his head and sat down at the table. "Warren Quade will live to be an old man and sure I pray that's true. But I can't wait that long, Tula Moon. Why do you torture me?"

Neither spoke for a moment. Roan watched his thumb as it traced creases in the knuckles of his other hand.

Tula remained by the fireplace. Finally she said, "I understand, my heart. I never meant to hurt you. I, too, have been in torment."

He looked up at her and shouted, "You've been killing yourself and me also." Gaining his feet, he faced her, his voice lowered to barely above a whisper. "I can't help you." His eyes misted.

Tula, her own eyes filled with tears, moved a step toward him, but he held up his hand to stop her. "I'll be leaving, Tula. I'm going back to me own land, back to Ireland. Might be I can get peace in me heart from your memory."

"Then I'll go with you, Roan."

He stared at her. "And how will you be doing that?"

"Warren Quade released me."

"He did what?"

"Long ago, I told you I would stay with Warren Quade as long as he needed me. It was my obligation, the way of my people."

"Aye," Roan replied. He was suddenly afraid to draw a breath.

"I spoke to Warren as you asked me to," Tula said. "He released me."

"Does this mean you no longer owe the man?"

She nodded. "In his own words, he said I was to follow my desires. He's a good man, Roan. He knew my heart. He wanted me to follow its leading. He told me something else, too."

"And what might that be?"

"He said he was building a house and we were to come back and live in it. Would that please you, spirit-of-my-life?"

Roan studied the flush on her olive skin and knew he must look the same way. "Would it please you?" he asked.

She moved a step toward him. "I know cultures, laws and even some religions change, have changed, Roan. But mine is the same as it has always been and always will be. I knew of no way to get around it and, because of it, I nearly lost you. My love for you lives deep in my heart's canyons. Do I want to go back to my people's land and live with you? Yes. But more than that, Roan McCrae, I want you." Tears wavered on the brims of her eyes, glittering there.

Roan folded her close to him and kissed the salty droplets as they spilled down her cheeks. "Tula Moon, it's not much you'll be getting and that's a fact, but me heart and soul are yours for the rest of me life."

He sought her soft, moist lips and tasted the sweetness there. As her heartbeat blended with his, the darkness in his soul burst into a world of bright light.

And in the distance, so far away he thought maybe he heard it only in his heart, a wolf howled . . . and his mate answered.